Also by
Molly Owen

A Leslie LaRue Mystery Series:
 #1: The Lost Medallion
 #2: The Antique Clock
 #3: The Sapphire Ring
 #4: The Cookbook

The Red Lady Inn

Molly Owen

I dedicate this book to my friends, Gene and Evelyn, who introduced me to their cabin on Beaver Lake, and my buddies, DiAnn, Teresa, and the late Deanna, as we enjoyed time together shopping and eating lunch at the Tea Room in Eureka Springs.

The Red Lady Inn

ACKNOWLEDGMENTS

Many trips to Eureka Springs in the early days with my late husband where we frequently stayed in the original two-room cabin that anchored a motor court on Highway 62 called Sherwood Courts, was the start of building memories in this unique place tucked away in the Ozark Mountains of Arkansas. More recently, after moving to the Ozarks, I explored the many attractions including, but not limited to, Christ of the Ozarks, the Crescent Hotel, the Passion Play and many wonderful Art galleries with friends. Each visit provides more fuel with memories of artists, shopkeepers, proprietors, and restaurant owners. It's a place filled with many different choices of cuisines from catfish, Mexican, the best hamburgers, tea rooms, to special meals in the dining hall at the Crescent Hotel or on the dining car of a train.

Molly Owen

I can't forget how my friend's cabin on Beaver lake inspired the story in this book. I hope you enjoy this journey with me as we travel the winding streets and whimsical houses on memory lane.

*Chapter **1***

A few miles from the historic tourist town of Eureka Springs, Arkansas on a small arm of Beaver Lake, Krista watched ripples forming circles in the water. She listened to the many melodies from different species of birds singing in tandem, answering each other simultaneously competing with each call as if to elevate it above the others.

Sudden sounds of rustling leaves shifted her attention to the path below the deck of the cabin deep in the woods. Her gaze locked into the large round, clear, brown eyes of a mature doe with white-tipped ears standing at attention while her reddish-brown body stood frozen on the path.

The two females stared at one another for a brief moment then Krista watched as the perfectly camouflaged animal sprinted between the trees, whitetail in the air, back into the dense woods. Squirrels scampered up and around the large oak tree, hugging the trunk, blending their grayish fur with like-colored bark, as the deer hooves thundered past them.

The forest surrounding the cabin would soon be naked as the leaves, in a plethora of colors, began to let go of their host and float effortlessly to the ground only to swirl upward again carried by a light breeze. Everywhere she looked seemed to let her know that even though life was flourishing among the wildlife, in and among the trees and beneath the water just feet from her, it would soon begin its winter hibernation and, with the hunting and fishing, some of the creatures would be lost, gone forever.

A shiver came over her as her short carrot red hair blew in the gentle breeze. In the distance, where the sun was descending behind the thick woods, the faint sound of barking dogs came across the water. *Hunters*, she thought as she remembered the large brown eyes of the doe looking deep into her soul sharing her pain. *Run sweetheart run.*

"So the doe didn't get your attention but the dogs did, is that right girl?" she said patting the head of Goldie, her golden retriever lying by her side. Her faithful companion raised her eyes and looked mournfully at her master.

"I wish the hunters didn't have to kill the deer, they are such beautiful creatures."

Insects began their serenade competing with the tree frogs as fireflies with their tiny beacons flashing on and off danced all around her, in and out of the shadows that drifted over the water, then over the cabin announcing it would soon be dark. *Father, I praise you, and thank you for the beauty that surrounds me. Thank you for your daily blessings. Be with me Lord Jesus in my decisions tomorrow. In Your Name. Amen.*

Leaving the comfort of the deck, she turned to take one final look into the woods, then motioned to Goldie. Opening the screen door into the primitive cabin, she followed her faithful companion inside. Untying her boots, she placed them next to the door and slipped into her house shoes. Pulling the hanging string cord, the bare bulb became the luminary for the small compact kitchen.

"Soup sounds good," Krista said. "How about you girl, are you hungry?" As she cranked the can opener on a can of Friskies, Goldie wagged her tail and stood obediently waiting for Krista to put her bowl on the floor. "There you go," she said, setting the bowl down.

Opening a can of gumbo soup, she poured the contents into a saucepan and striking a match, lit the propane burner on the stove. She looked through the cabinet for the crackers, kept them in a sealed container, then laid the red and white checked placemat along with the crackers on the handmade table Drew had fashioned in his workshop behind the cabin.

"There, that'll do just fine," again speaking the words aloud but aware of the emptiness around her now normal, however, still lonely life. Gazing into the twilight through the large-paned window facing the deck, flashbacks of memories filled her mind.

*****

Drew, with the help of his friends, spent weekends and holidays building the log cabin from the logs cleared on the land then chopped and split to the right lengths according to the plans he sent for out of a Woodsman magazine. Krista remembered the times spent in a tent cooking on a camp stove as Drew's dream became a reality over the year and a half. The next two years found Drew in his workshop building furniture for their home away from home. Krista, a loan bank officer and Drew a stockbroker owned a historic house in downtown Rogers they called home. The cabin gave them a place to escape the busy lives they lived, a place to relax, read, fish, enjoy the peace and quiet of the secluded location. They talked about traveling or buying a fancy boat, each idea they came up with interfered with the life they already enjoyed.

"Why should we change things if everything is perfect the way it is?" Drew had said before they made the decision to invest the inheritance left to her by her father, putting it away for a rainy day or their old age.

*****

Deep in her soul, the pain lingered. They would never grow old together, she thought, but maybe now was the time to use the rainy day money to help her move on with her life. She had come to the cabin to think, after seeing an ad in the paper early Sunday morning. The bed and breakfast where she and Drew spent their honeymoon would auction off Monday in Eureka Springs. The tour of the three-story building would begin at eight in the morning and the auction would take place at two in the afternoon. Krista wanted that building. She wanted to run the bed and breakfast holding the memories of those five wonderful days spent in the Honeymoon Suite with the large Jacuzzi they enjoyed while the snow blew around outside filling the corners of the paned-windows in their room. Memories of that time brought warmth to her heart as she recalled spending hours in front of the fireplace sharing one large blanket while drinking hot chocolate.

Reaching in her pocket, she took out her cell phone and called her boss, Sandy, at home.

"Hi, Krista, what's up?" Sandy asked.

"Well, I came to the cabin to think and I have made an important decision. Remember the old Inn in Eureka Springs I told you about, well, I'm going to bid on it at an auction and I'm pretty sure I'll win the bid," she told Sandy, "Could I have a couple of days to complete the deal?"

"No problem, I hope it works out for you Krista, let me know as soon as the auction is over."

Molly Owen

"Oh, I will, and thank you."

*****

She and Sandy were more than co-workers, they were close friends, and Sandy was excited to see Krista doing something constructive. She had watched her over the past two years go through all the stages of grieving. For the most part, Krista had handled things very well, considering Drew was her life. His sudden death left everyone uneasy knowing the same thing could happen at any moment to any of them. A young healthy active man, full of life, happy, smart, excellent at his job, one day without warning gone from a brain aneurysm. When Krista called her from the hospital, Sandy could not believe what she heard.

"Sandy, I'm at the hospital, could you come and get me? Drew is gone." Krista had said so calmly Sandy was not sure she heard right.

Drew gone? It had not made sense to her, how could that happen to someone like him, she questioned. Sandy had always been a come-what-may type of person, knowing God was in charge she never questioned Him, however, this threw her into a period of re-evaluation of her beliefs. She depended on her faith to get her through the rough spots, and now she felt uneven like standing sideways on a hill.

The drive to the hospital that day filled her mind with questions and found her not knowing what she could say to help Krista. Upon her arrival, she found Krista sitting in a waiting room full of people, babies crying, kids running everywhere, people coughing, and obviously sick all around her, and yet she did not seem to notice. Sandy went to her and sat in the chair beside her. Krista looked at her with a blank stare as if she did not recognize her. The look on Krista's face haunted Sandy for several weeks.

In the following months, Sandy watched her friend, Krista, deal with this devastation with grace and dignity full of faith and wondered how she held it together. There had been moments when Krista would cry unexpectedly, which Sandy knew was normal, but she became concerned that Krista was holding back her grief, afraid to show any weakness. So she was pleased that Krista was looking to the future with renewed interest.

*****

The aroma of boiling soup brought Krista temporarily back to the present as she poured the steaming liquid into the bowl and set it on the placemat. One of the loneliest parts of the day was eating a meal. It was supposed to be something shared, preferably with your spouse sitting across the table as you had light conversations about the events of the day or in the morning the plans for your day. *It's not supposed to be this way,* she thought and she was unable to reconcile the other question that came to the surface occasionally. As much as her faith was tested, she trusted her Lord and Savior with her whole being, however, she found grieving to be very hard work and sometimes overwhelming. These times she would go to prayer, letting God take her burden.

With her dinner finished, she washed and dried the bowl and spoon, putting them in the cupboard. The hot soup tasted good and now she was ready for a cup of tea while relaxing with a good book. The steam from the teakettle whistled and Krista poured the hot water over the teabag. Pulling the string up and down until the liquid turned the right color she wrapped the string around her spoon and squeezed out the rest of the liquid, she added a squirt of lemon from a plastic lemon-shaped container and a teaspoon of real sugar she kept in an airtight jar. Each mundane movement filled her time and mind. Carefully, she carried the tea down the step into the main room of the cabin, setting it on the table, she sat down in the big chair with soft pillows. Propping her feet on the three-legged footstool, she picked up the book she was reading, one of Nicolas Sparks' latest, and settle back for a restful evening, pretending Drew was next to her on the couch reading his woodworking book while Goldie was curled up on the braided rug next to the chair.

Two hours later, her eyes burned from the strain of reading beyond concentration. Laying the book down, she went to the door and let Goldie out and waited until she returned, letting her in. After shutting and locking the door, she checked the back door and turned out the lights. Making her way in the dark, with Goldie following her every move, she turned the light on in the bathroom and brushed her teeth, then climbed the steps to the loft bedroom. Dressing in her warm flannel pajamas she took a quilt from the trunk at the end of the bed, expecting the night air to cool down, she threw it on top of the other covers, then pulled back the layers of warm materials and crawled in. Her eyes focused on the picture next to the bed and she blew a kiss to Drew, told him goodnight, turned off the lamp, and snuggled under the covers pulling all of them up close under her chin. Goldie circled a couple of times in her bed on the floor. Laying her head down, she sighed. Once Goldie settled, Krista said, "Let's pray." This was their normal routine; however, they were both acutely aware that Drew was not there with them. *"Heavenly Father, I'm so blessed by your grace. You surround me daily giving me hope for the future. I pray I'm making the right decision, Lord. Give me strength and courage for things to come. I love you, God. In Jesus' Name, Amen"*

Eyelids closed, her mind continued to produce pictures of the past, drifting in and out of sleep, she recalled sitting on the boat dock competing with Drew to catch the biggest fish. He would smile as she pulled in a big bass. They would weigh and measure and more times than not, she would win the competition, which she suspected secretly pleased him since he had taught her everything she knew about fishing. After much tossing and turning, she was finally able to fall into a deep sleep.

Chapter 2

Standing in the doorway to the Honeymoon Suite, she was surprised the room had changed so much in the past seven years. *I'll put it back exactly as it was before,* she thought with a quick peek at the bathroom with the large claw foot tub, pedestal sink, and cute décor. She stopped in front of the Jacuzzi still sitting in the middle of the room remembering one cold winter snowy day seven years ago. Wiping away a tear, she went down the hall and examined the other bedrooms. Upstairs the living quarters were ample for one person, rather cozy more like the cabin than the big house she now called home. She liked the quaint kitchen with the bar, noting there was no room for a table and chairs. Downsizing would definitely be in order however, she saw no problem with it as long as she could use her antique furniture in other parts of the bed and breakfast.

Overall, she was happy with her decision and planned to be back in the afternoon for the auction.

After getting a bite to eat, she drove around Eureka Springs and took the house tour, as Drew referred to it, along Spring Street. The streets wove in and out around curves up and down hills and each section revealed a different architecture, color, style, making the whole scene eclectic. She and Drew had often talked of moving to Eureka Springs but loved their old historic house in Rogers and being close to work. Now her plan was to quit her job, rent out her house, live at the Inn, take the winter to revitalize the rooms, and open under a new name in the spring. She knew Drew would approve, her only wish was that they could have shared it together.

That afternoon, as expected, she outbid the other investors and began arranging for the closing. Since she would pay cash, the sale would go rather quickly and the present owners would need to vacate as soon as possible. She felt such excitement over her newfound life that it scared her a little. Was she letting go of Drew? Would her memories fade as she had feared from the beginning? Would she forget his expressions, the twinkle in his eyes when he teased her? She could not let that happen but sensed a transition taking place that she was not sure she was ready to experience.

This time she toured the house alone and investigated every nook and cranny making mental notes as she went along trying to locate places for the extra furniture she would bring. Her head was spinning with ideas while she walked down the stairs to the street-level gift shop. As she walked through the shop, she came upon the present owner, an older woman perhaps in her late sixties with her salt and pepper grey hair tied up on the crown of her head in a bun, her face round with sparkling eyes and a smile that greeted Krista at once.

"Well, what do you think? I bet you see some changes that need making and I have a feeling you're just the one to bring this old lady back to life, referring of course to the Inn," Mrs. Schmidt said with a chuckle.

"I can't tell you how excited I am to own this magnificent place. Are you sad to be leaving?" Krista said, brimming over with enthusiasm.

"Yes, we'll miss it, but it's time to move on. We're not getting any younger and this place ties you down so, we're going to do some traveling and then settle closer to our children and grandchildren," she told Krista then continued. "Have you had any experience running an Inn?"

"No, I'm a banker, so this will all be new to me, I hope you'll be available to fill me in on some things as I go along," Krista remarked.

"Well, we're fortunate to have an association of business people here and they're very supportive of each other. You'll get lots of help in that direction, sometimes it's hard to keep good help with the everyday upkeep but don't worry, you'll work it out I'm sure," Mrs. Schmidt told her not wanting to scare her but preparing her for a few hurdles as she took ownership.

"Looking over the financials, the gift shop just about breaks even, has it always been that way?" Krista observed casually.

"I don't want you to think you have bought a white elephant, however, my husband's health is not what it was when we first bought this place ten years ago. The past two years have been difficult and I'm afraid we've not had the passion we did in the beginning. You're young and I'm sure you'll bring this wonderful place back to the way it's meant to be, romantic, exciting, and fun."

"You probably don't remember," Krista said, suddenly feeling sorrow as she swallowed and held her breath to keep tears at bay, then continuing, "my husband and I spent our honeymoon here almost eight years ago this coming November. We were the only guest you had and it snowed the whole five days."

"I do remember. My goodness, imagine that, and now you will own the very place you spent your honeymoon. How wonderful," Mrs. Schmidt said, not wanting to pry as to the whereabouts of Krista's husband. "If I recall right you were going to live in Rogers in an old historic place downtown, so do you still live there?"

"Drew, my husband, died quite suddenly, almost two years ago of a brain aneurysm," Krista said in answer to the unasked question.

"I'm so sorry to hear that dear, it must be very hard for you," Mrs. Schmidt said sincerely putting her hand on Krista's shoulder.

Krista did not answer but looked away to hide the tears spilling over her eyelids. Touched by the women's genuine concern for her pain brought her deep emotions to the surface. It was even more difficult as she realized her own mother would be around Mrs. Schmidt's age had she lived. That was the missing link in all of her grief. Both her parents were gone and she had no brothers or sisters to turn to in her hours of grief. Now, this kind compassionate woman was filling that void.

"It's alright dear, to show your emotions, my goodness you have lost the love of your life and you have a right to grieve," Mrs. Schmidt said putting her arms around Krista and hugging her, swaying a little back and forth she patted her back as a mother with a child.

Krista sobbed uncontrollably, and then as Mrs. Schmidt took her to a chair to sit down, Krista poured her pent-up feelings to this virtual stranger. She told her about the cabin and the inheritance. She told her how awful it was to wake up every day knowing she could not touch him, hear his voice, laugh at his jokes, hold his hand, and kiss him.

Molly Owen

"I miss his hugs and the way he told me he loved me," she said with an unfamiliar voice in between sobs, "it's so hard to watch couples holding hands without a care in the world if they only knew how precious that time is together."

"I understand dear, your world is not the same and I imagine the hardest part is putting it in the past and making a new world for yourself. Is that why you wanted to buy this place? Because of the memories, it held for you?" the older woman asked

"Drew and I loved Eureka Springs and we often talked about living here and running a bed and breakfast. I honestly think he would be pleased with my decision to buy this place. In all my excitement about it, I can feel his presence here and I think it will fill my lonely days with wonderful plans and help me move into the future," she said, wiping her face with the tissue Mrs. Schmidt had given her.

"I think you're right dear, this is just what you need, something to sink your teeth into, as they say. It will be a challenge and a lot of hard work but I think you're ready for a change of scenery. I believe you made the right decision and I'm very proud of you for being so courageous," she said patting Krista's hands that lay in her lap.

"Thank you, thank you so much for affirming me and for listening, you're very kind. I just wish you were staying around here. I could use a good friend," Krista told her.

"Well, we'll be around for a while, we bought a cottage out on highway twenty-three and it will be our base when we start traveling," Mrs. Schmidt said with an encouraging smile. "And sweetie you can call me anytime, we can have lunch and girl talk and I'll try to get you up to speed on the business of running an Inn."

Returning to the car after one last look around, she opened the door and let Goldie out. "Come on girl, this is our new home, I know you will love the woods around here and the new smells in the garden. Oh, Goldie, it is going to be so much fun," she said down on her knees hugging her companion around her furry neck.

She could not wait to call Sandy and let her know all about her plans. She wanted to tell her how Mrs. Schmidt was so wonderful and how she confirmed her decision to buy the Inn. She felt alive again as if a burden lifted from her shoulders and she was free to enjoy again for the first time in over a year. As much as she hated to leave, she knew she needed to get back to Rogers. There was so much to do, give notice at the bank, sell or lease her house, pack and get ready to move.

"Come on girl," she said letting Goldie back in the car.

Her mind raced as she envisioned the changes she anticipated making over the next few months. Driving along highway sixty-two she automatically braked for the tight curves as the sun began to set behind the hills in the Ozarks. She wondered how difficult it was going to be to find a contractor to work through the winter at the Inn. It would need to be local because no one would want to travel these roads in the winter, she thought. Finding the right person would be her top priority. Perhaps the Schmidts would recommend someone.

Arriving back home, and after letting Goldie out, she hurried in to call her friend. Sorting through the mail she heard Sandy answer.

"Sandy, I'm back and I got the Inn. I'm so excited about it and the present owners are wonderful people and they will help me get started," she rambled on without taking a breath.

Sandy listened intently to every word not wanting to interrupt and not wanting to bring into the conversation any negatives, but she did have some concerns. She was elated to hear Krista's enthusiasm and she was happy beyond words for her, however, some misgivings had crossed her mind from the beginning. She knew how confining this kind of business could be and hoped that Krista was ready to put her whole life into this endeavor. On the other hand, maybe this was just what the doctor ordered. Mrs. Schmidt sounded like a levelheaded kind person that Krista could count on to guide her through.

"So I'm giving my two-week notice at the bank tomorrow, then I'll start packing," Krista concluded, switching the phone receiver to the other ear.

"What are you going to do with the house?" Sandy asked

"I'm not sure. I may lease it."

"Would you put it with a leasing agent?"

"That would probably be the smart thing to do."

Sandy hadn't told Krista her own plans to own a real estate agency. She had taken and passed her real estate broker's license test, and saved enough money to fulfill her own dreams. She wasn't ready to discuss it but knew that being the agent for Krista's house would get her off to a start. As Manager of the branch bank in Rogers, she had many contacts but her timeline would be behind Krista's, as she needed time to close the deal on the agency she planned to buy and hire some realtors. She would wait to talk to her about it, so Krista could have her excitement without having to share the limelight.

"Krista, I've got to go get Brad from football practice, I'll see you in the morning," Sandy told her, assuring her she could call later with more details if she wanted.

Divorced, with two teenagers headed for college, Sandy was determined to work for herself and increase her income. It was a risk, but one she had to take if she were to have enough money to put her kids through college. She already owned a couple of rental properties and hoped to purchase several more houses as they became available before they went on the market.

Two single women branching out on their own, how awesome, challenging, and scary, Sandy thought as she set the alarm and locked the door to the bank.

Chapter 3

oxes everywhere reminded Krista that she brought entirely too much stuff, even for the three-story Inn. She ran up and downstairs looking for things belonging in her living quarters then she became more distracted by opening a box that belonged on the second floor or in storage. Anxious to begin moving she was packing before the movers arrived and started taking boxes of things to Eureka and unloading them on the first floor. "I should have let the movers do all the packing, at least I would know what room it came from," she said aloud.

Goldie was lying on the floor next to Krista when she suddenly stood up on all four legs, ears straight up and tail wagging.

Molly Owen

"Ms. Moore, I presume," this deep male voice from behind her stated.

Getting up and turning around she came face to face with a tall, tanned, well-built, sandy-haired individual and she found herself pushing her hair from her face and pulling on her wrinkled clothes hoping to be more presentable. Before she could speak, he reached down and pat Goldie on the head, then he extended his hand and introduced himself, "I hope you don't mind, but the door was open. My name is Jack, short for Jackson, the last name is Nolan," he said with a smile that covered most of his face. "Mrs. Schmidt said you may need some handyman work done and I'm here to apply for the job."

"Well, Mr. Nolan, if Mrs. Schmidt sent you then I'm sure you're hired. I trust her judgment completely," she said firmly not wanting her five feet four inches to reduce her power or control of the situation. "And Goldie seems to also approve," she said, patting the dog's tail wagging backside with her one free hand.

Smiling down at her from his lofty six feet three inches, he let go of her hand and looked around the room. She pushed the hair behind her ears and smoothed the front of her shirt again. *What are you doing?* she asked herself nervously.

"I won't charge you for carrying these boxes to where they need to go and we can talk about what you need to be done, then I'll give you some idea about the kind of work I can do, how does that sound? By the way, please, just call me Jack," he remarked.

Taken by surprise, she told him to call her Krista and they began moving boxes to their proper places after opening each one to study its contents. They talked about what she had in mind for the Inn and he told her his skills varied, ranging from carpentry to masonry. She asked him if he thought it would probably take most of the winter to get the Inn ready to open in the spring. He agreed and suggested she pays him a salary and he would be available on a daily basis to help with painting, wallpapering, cleaning, building, plumbing, electrical, and even building the walkways in the garden as she had suggested. He was used to a steady income and worked for a construction company in the summer so this would take him through the winter. They agreed on a wage, she told him to start the next day and that payday was the end of each week.

"I'll give you a key and a list of items I need to be done. I'll have to go back to Rogers a few times to complete paperwork and so forth, but outside of that I'll be here every day." Krista said, carrying a lamp, as they climbed the stairs to her quarters. "Just put that box in the other room please, and how about a drink?"

"Sounds good, water will be fine," he said surveying her living quarters. "This will be nice when you get it done."

"I'd like to start up here, so at the end of the day I'd have a nice place to retreat and rest from the day's activities, however, it's probably not at the top of the priority list," she said, handing him a glass of ice water. "Here, take a seat," she said, moving some items from the kitchen barstool.

"Thank you, so what brings you to Eureka Springs?" he asked, pulling the stool up to the bar.

"The opportunity to own and run this Inn," she said, not wanting to share her history with a person she had just met although he made her feel at ease and he was easy to talk to. "How about you, how long have you lived here?"

"I grew up in these parts, over in Berryville up on Highway sixty-two, but I've lived here in Eureka for about six years. I built a little place out of ways from town back in the woods." Jack told her.

She thought about telling him about the cabin on Beaver Lake and saved it for another time thinking he had given enough of his time to her for one day and probably needed to leave. After a little more conversation, Jack got off the stool and put his glass in the sink.

"Thank you for the job and the ice water, I'll be back in the morning at nine o'clock sharp ready to work."

After he left, Krista placed a call to Mrs. Schmidt to thank her for sending Jack her way.

"He's such a nice man, dear, and I know he does good work, we hired him several times to fix things and he always did a great job and quick too." Mrs. Schmidt told her. "When I had to take Mr. Schmidt to the doctor, and then when he was in the hospital, Jack took care of the Inn, he would sleep on a cot behind the counter so we would not have to cancel reservations. He's very trustworthy, helping anywhere he can."

*****

Thankful for winter income, Jack went over in his mind the things Krista wanted to happen at the Inn. Impressed by Krista's professionalism and her decorating knowledge, he still wondered why a young woman would tie herself down to running a bed and breakfast type operation. The Schmidts were a couple and able to share the responsibility but Krista according to Elsa Schmidt, was single, or as she put it alone. Whatever the reason for her buying the Inn, he was excited to be working with her to renovate the old building and it did not hurt one bit that she was a looker, smart too.

*****

Relieved that she had already been able to hire good help she went downstairs and began to empty boxes. Each item brought back memories as she carefully unwrapped the treasures she and Drew had lived with since their marriage. When she came to the box of framed pictures she hesitated then sat down on the floor and slowly began to take each one out and examine it. She had not seen this particular box of pictures since Drew died. She had taken them down from the walls where they hung and packed them away because they were too painful to see. Most of the pictures were of her or Drew and all of their wedding pictures but at the bottom of the box were framed pictures of her mom and dad. After looking at each one, she made two piles, one to go back in the box and the other she would hang on the walls in her quarters. She repacked the box and marked it to go in storage then took the rest of the boxed items upstairs.

Climbing three flights of stairs to her little corner of the world, she suddenly felt very lonely. She longed to have the companionship; the evenings spent talking about the day, making plans for the future, things that seemed so normal, and yet she wondered if she would ever have that again. Putting the pictures down, she reached into her pocket for her cell phone.

"Hi Sandy, do you have time to talk?"

"Sure, what's up?"

"Well, I hired a handyman today and he starts work tomorrow morning. Mrs. Schmidt recommended him. She says he's very reliable and trustworthy."

"That's wonderful Krista."

"He seems very nice, maybe in his thirties, nice looking, by the way. When he came to the Inn, I didn't hear him come in, and it startled me when he spoke, then when I turned around, I was not two feet from him. He's very tall, taller than Drew was maybe six feet two or three inches and has a slow drawl that could melt butter. Anyway, my reaction to him kinda surprised me."

"You mean you were attracted to him?"

"Well, sorta... in a weird way."

"And what's wrong with that?"

"He's going to be here every day and I don't want anything to interfere with getting the Inn ready by spring. He says it's doable and I sure hope he's right."

"I think it's normal for you to find someone attractive and I understand your concern, however, I think you should just take one day at a time," Sandy said secretly hoping that Krista could find someone to fill the void left by Drew's death.

"You're probably right, I just want everything to run smoothly and he appears to be very anxious to do the work and who knows he may have a girlfriend and even be married. Oh, what am I saying I don't want to get involved with anyone; that's absurd."

She still held the cell phone in her hand trying to process the conversation that had just ended but she had a queasy feeling in her stomach like when you think you have done something wrong. Her talk with Sandy only clarified what she was afraid she was feeling and now she felt a strong sense of betrayal even knowing that Drew was gone forever and it would not be sinful to remarry, she was still having a hard time getting used to the many emotions that surrounded her.

Closing the cell phone, she bowed her head, *Thank you Lord for the opportunity to purchase the Inn, and Father guide me as I deal with my emotions as Jack and I begin work on the Inn. In Jesus' Name. Amen*

Chapter **4**

For the past several weeks, Krista had returned to Rogers, and then to the cabin to check on things and move some of the items from the house in Rogers to the storeroom behind the cabin. Returning on Sunday afternoon, she would prepare for the week ahead by lining up jobs for Jack and making a list of the projects, she needed him to work on.

One Sunday evening, she sat in her new living room contemplating the direction she wanted her quarters to take as far as color, she loved the jewel tones and although the white walls enlarged the place, she felt a drastic change would do her soul good. She was aware that up until now she had leaned toward the conservative in her life. Maybe the time had come to take more chances and break out of her cocoon. She would start with the kitchen... granite countertops, *was that too drastic?* she thought. *Maybe Jack could help her with this.*

Her thoughts went back to the past few days as she and Jack saw each other every day. *Why am I so comfortable with him?* Nothing like Drew, who was of Italian descent, dark hair, dark eyes, Jack was more Swedish in appearance, sandy hair, blue eyes, soft-spoken. Drew, on the other hand, was strong, sure of himself, and in charge. With her Irish shining like a beacon, red hair, temper and all, she had always attracted people of a hard disposition, not cold but more in control of things and people around them. This man was soft, gentle and even with his large stature seemed cuddly as a bear. He deferred to her ideas and wishes and never tried to overpower her with his own opinion but expressed himself in a way that got her attention.

He had become her teacher, showing her how to take care of fuses, shut-offs, water heater pilots, switch to the generator, all the things she never knew anything about until now. His patience with her inexperience was refreshing. Patience had not been Drew's virtue especially when it came to teaching Krista about man's work, therefore he was content for Krista to sit and watch. Jack taught her different tools and their usage and let her do some of the work under his supervision. He encouraged her to learn.

"You never know when you may need to know these things. The winters can be pretty harsh with snow and ice and I may not be able to get here, so the more you know about taking care of this ole lady, the better," Jack had told her. "Minor repairs could probably wait until I got here but a busted pipe, a power outage would need to be taken care of pretty fast."

"I do appreciate you showing me these things, Jack, I never thought I would need to know all of this but, as you say, I may not be able to rely on you," she had told him, remembering his crystal blue eyes looking at her.

"I've been meaning to ask if you're going to Rogers this weekend," Jack asked.

"I was planning to stay here, I'm pretty well out of the house and my friend Sandy is going to start showing it. Why?" diverting her eyes away from his, she had asked hesitantly, not knowing if she was ready for a personal relationship.

"I just wanted to put in a plug for my church up on Spring Street, it isn't a very large congregation and with a smaller group, it would be easy to get to know people. The Schmidts go there also and if you've not made a decision about your new church home, I wish you would give us a try,"

"Well, I just may do that, Jack Nolan, I need to get back into a church, I've attended church almost every Sunday since Drew died, at first it was hard but as time went by it became easier," she had confided in him. "Yes, I need to find a church home here, thank you for telling me about yours, I'll try it out," she had said, still not ready to commit to anything beyond a working situation.

Molly Owen

"Do they have a good choir?" she had asked.

"Well, I think we do, but I'll let you be the judge of that," he had said with a grin.

Returning to the present, she began to follow her nightly routine, letting Goldie out and back in, making sure all systems are shut down, then finally setting the alarm and lights out. This routine gave her peace somehow, made her aware of her surroundings so that sleep would come easily. However, this night she found herself thinking more and more about the previous happenings as she compared her past life with her present life. Thankful for a change, a new beginning as such. Before allowing her mind to shut off, she thanked God again for the blessings knowing He was beside her always through the unexpected changes giving her the peace she yearned for. *Heavenly Father, thank you for guiding me, through the Holy Spirit, and thank you for the blessings of this opportunity and for bringing me a Christian to help with this project. You bring me peace and hope for my future God and I'm so grateful. In Jesus' Name, Amen.* Soon she was sound asleep, only to live in her dreams, this time more about Jack and less about Drew.

*****

Jack was aware of the emotional merry-go-round Krista was experiencing. He remembered very well the insecurity, the out-of-control emotions, and the unwillingness to commit to any relationship. He did not want to push Krista into anything she could not handle emotionally, however, he felt her need to be with fellow believers. They didn't talk about it much but he knew she was a believer by her actions. He noticed her bible sometimes on the table when he was in her quarters. One day she had sent him to her kitchen to get the plumbing supplies she bought the day before. He saw her open Bible next to a notebook where she had recorded some scriptures. He remembered his own attempt to search out answers to his questions after Debbie died.

Jack and Debbie were married a short time when she discovered a lump in her breast. The next year was difficult as her stage four cancer metastasized. She went through chemotherapy after surgery to remove her breasts but the disease still spread. She began to lose the battle, and shortly after their fourth anniversary, she was gone. That was six years ago and the memory still haunted him.

He had spent the next few months building his place in the woods appreciating the solitude that gave him time to heal. The move to Eureka Springs had been a good decision. He became part of the community, building friendships and when not working, volunteering for different projects through the church. His faith had kept him going and he saw that faith was the beacon that kept Krista going.

Slowly, Krista was opening up to him, sharing some of her past with him. She talked endlessly about Drew, as expected, but lately not so much. She told him about their cabin and how like himself, Drew was a craftsman. He felt like he knew Sandy personally although they had never met. Until now, Jack had not shared much about himself, as he was a good listener when Krista needed to talk. He knew she would heal in her own time and he was not about to rush it. Therefore, he listened and waited.

*****

"Hello," Krista answered, drying her hands on a paper towel and holding the receiver between her ear and shoulder.

"Hello dear, this is Mrs. Schmidt, we would love for you to attend church with us Sunday and if it is alright with you, we will stop by for you around 9:15. Will that work?"

"I believe so. But I don't want to put you out any," Krista said, holding the receiver in her hand, a little curious as to how they knew she was going to attend their church and why Jack had not offered to take her.

"Not at all, dear, we're happy to have you, see you on Sunday,"

Krista was becoming more confused every day about her feelings towards Jack. She liked him as a person and was glad he was a believer, but she did not understand her reactions where he was concerned. Did she or did she not want him to see her as potential dating material and why was she upset that he had not asked to take her to his church. She felt a little hurt that he asked the Schmidts to take her although it was very sweet of them, could he not do it himself, she wondered.

The Red Lady Inn

The Inn, built in the rock of the mountain, was like many other buildings in Eureka Springs that had entrances on two separate streets, one above and the other below. Her living quarters on the top floor faced the upper street while the Inn's Gift Shop and entrance for registration in the Bed and Breakfast faced the lower street. She sat in the rocker on her porch and watched the squirrels scamper in the leaves across the street. Soon the Schmidts drove up and carrying her bible, she bid them a cheery good morning then letting Goldie back in the house shut the door. She got in their car and sat in the back seat. There was polite chatter among the three of them en route to the church.

"Does Goldie have enough room to roam?"

"Oh, yes and she loves chasing squirrels in the garden and running through the leaves."

"She's a beautiful dog, how do you keep her coat so shiny?"

"Well, like it or not she gets a bath every Saturday."

Soon they pulled to the front door of the church. Mr. Schmidt, a quiet sort with more hair on his face than his head, let the two women out while he parked the car. They entered the sanctuary, found their seat close to the front, the whole time Mrs. Schmidt introducing Krista first to one and then another until they sat down, leaving room for Mr. Schmidt who soon arrived and scooted in beside his wife.

Krista looked up as the organ began to play and the small choir entered followed by the director and the pastors. She could not believe her eyes. Was that Jack in the choir robe? Then she realized he was the choir director and had never said a word about it. *That is why he didn't ask to bring me,* she thought. *Well, wait until I tell him I sing, and want to be in the choir.*

After the service, the Schmidts led Krista downstairs to the fellowship hall for coffee and cookies where Jack caught up with them.

"So, what do you think? Do we have a good choir?" Jack asked, coming up behind her.

"You think you're pretty smart, Jack Nolan, don't you? By the way, I've always sung in the choir, so when is practice?" Krista grinned at him.

"Wednesday nights 6:00 o'clock sharp and for that, I can take you," he said knowing she wondered why he had not offered to take her to church. "I told the Schmidts I could take you home, that is, if it's alright with you. I thought we might stop by and get something to eat on our way."

Krista agreed without hesitation and asked if they could eat at a place she had heard about, out on highway sixty-two "Of course that's an excellent choice, all the locals eat there and you're a local after all," he said teasing her.

They walked out to the church parking lot and Jack introduced her to several of the choir members telling them she would soon be joining their little group. Once in Jack's truck, he asked her what part she sang. "Either second soprano or alto, I have a limited range, not too high and not too low, if you know what I mean and don't even suggest a solo I'm a choir singer, not a soloist," she answered as they pulled out of the parking lot and headed for the highway.

Sitting across the table from each other, they searched the menu. "Any recommendations?" Krista asked.

"The hamburgers are the best and they come with lots of fries," Jack said, still engrossed in reading the menu. They both ordered the hamburger plate, handed their menus to the waiter, and settled into the booth as their drinks came, large coke with lime wedges.

After the server left, Jack looked up from his drinking straw and commented on how nice Krista looked all dressed up.

"You clean up pretty good yourself, Mr. Choir Director. I can not believe we have spent all this time together and you never mentioned that," she said, laughing.

"Now, I bet you may have not told me everything about yourself, such as the fact you have always sung in church choirs, now that gives us something in common, don't you think?" he said teasing her.

"I've rattled on about myself ever since we met and I still don't know much about you. Are you keeping any other secrets?"

"Oh, a few, but I'm sure the time will come when you'll know all of them," he said with a grin that put crinkles at the corners of his eyes.

Krista was not sure how old Jack was but guessed him to be in his thirties. He seemed mature and settled unlike most men that age. At thirty-two, she felt as though she had already lived a lifetime. Married as soon as she received her BA from the University of Tulsa, she felt as though she was married much longer than seven years,

"A penny for your thoughts," Jack asked softly watching Krista drain her drink with the slurp of the straw.

"I was wondering how old you are?" she said, not taking her eyes off of his face in case he thought about fudging a little.

"Is it important?"

"I guess not. I was thinking that I was married seven years of my adult life. I'm thirty-two," she said, waiting for him to respond.

"Well, you're just a kid. I'm thirty-eight, I spent five years in the service then came back and got my masters at the U of A in Fayetteville," he told her, grateful that their food had arrived and he need not reveal any more. He was not ready for the barrage of questions further information would bring and he was not sure if she was ready to hear about his pain.

They enjoyed the rest of their meal with small talk about the community and other things to do around town. "Most places shut down in the winter, even the restaurants because the tourist trade dries up as temperatures drop. Weather permitting, the exception could be keeping the shops open at Christmas. Even that presented issues. Unpredictable storms might make a surprise entrance costing shopkeepers money invested in merchandise. So, you have to know how to cook and be sure to stock up on groceries in case the stores close," he told her, again preparing her for living through the winter in Eureka Springs.

Not paying much attention, she processed the more pressing questions in her mind. *Was there a woman in his life? Why was he not married? What kind of experiences had he had to make him so perceptive? Did he fight in a battle while in the service?* So many questions but she knew he was not going to tell her anything until he was ready.

Chapter **5**

Wednesday nights became a routine. Jack took her to choir practice and afterward they would try a new place for supper, sometimes inviting others from the choir to join them. It was during one of those get-together evenings that Jack introduced her to a friend of his that happened to be at their favorite hangout.

"Krista, I would like you to meet Bud, he's a good friend of mine," Jack said as Bud pulled up a chair, turned it around, straddled the seat, and sat down with his arms crossed, resting on the back of the chair.

"Hello, I'm glad to finally meet you. Jack has told me a lot about you," Krista said to the much taller and broader version of Tom Cruise.

"All bad probably, but I've got a few stories to tell about him too," he said, giving Krista a big wink as if to let her know he would share anything she wanted to know. "So what's going on?" he said to Jack.

"Just hanging out, we had choir practice tonight and stopped to get something to eat," Jack replied, noticing how Bud looked at Krista.

She tossed her head back to get her hair that had grown almost to her shoulders, out of her face and then gave Bud a long look finally asking him if he had known Jack very long. For some reason, she felt she knew Bud from somewhere.

"Yeah, we went to school together," Bud told her then stopped short of telling her anything as Jack gave him the evil eye letting him know to keep his mouth shut.

"Bud is a fireman, Krista, he's also a paramedic and a pretty good guy to know in an emergency."

"I pray we won't need you, no offense, but I would rather run into you occasionally or socially if you don't mind," Krista smiled at him.

Having the feeling that there was more to Jack than she knew, she had a hard time keeping quiet and not asking many questions. She knew Bud was about to say something Jack did not want to reveal and that puzzled her because she was beginning to feel close to Jack and comfortable sharing her feelings with him. *Maybe it's a male thing*, she thought glancing over at him just as he looked her way.

Just then, Bud waved at some people arriving, said his goodbyes to Jack, and told Krista he hoped to see her again sometime.

"Bud was sweet on my sister when we were in High School," he said, filling the silence.

"Is he married," she asked. Jack shook his head and immediately changed the subject.

"I sure am glad you joined the choir, Krista, you have a good voice and the fact you read music helps the alto section. I've seen a real improvement since you joined, I've tried for a year or more to encourage young people to join us and when you joined the solo group, *viola*, we have new members. Mind you, I'm not complaining, just saying…"

"Just saying? What makes you think I had anything to do with it?"

"Because most of the new ones are in the bass and tenor section," he said, paying the cashier as they were leaving the café.

"So…?" She said with a closed smile and sheepish look standing beside him at the cash register.

He laughed and put his arm around her shoulders, gave her a little squeeze, then realizing what he had done he dropped his

Molly Owen

arm and went ahead of her to open the door holding it for her. Then he headed for the truck door and made sure she was in before shutting the door. Hurrying around to the other side he got in and avoided eye contact while backing out of the parking space onto the highway.

Krista noticed his attempt at covering up his jester but she chose to ignore it and after a few awkward moments started talking about the plans for tomorrow's jobs. It was not the first time he had touched her. When she almost fell from the ladder he was steadying, she slipped reaching for the box on the top shelf and he grabbed her around the waist. Then there were many times their hands almost met while using tools to hold pipes or hanging pictures but those were unintentional, this was an impulsive act, but not without feeling. She had to admit it felt good and she would not be sorry for it to happen again.

Pulling up in front of her door, he determined by her silence that he better leave well enough alone.

"It was a good practice tonight, Jack, would you like to come in for a while?" she said as they sat in his truck outside the Inn.

"Thanks, but I better get home, we have a lot of work to do tomorrow."

"As a matter of fact I should do some domestic chores myself and I better walk Goldie. Thank you for the ride and dinner."

"No sense in taking two cars when we work together, besides it gives us some personal time, I mean, time to know each other better, I mean not that we don't know each other but...."

Hoping to defuse the conversation and sensing his discomfort, she said. "It was nice meeting your friend Bud, he seems like a nice guy."

"Yes, he can be a pain sometimes but we have been friends forever. Do you want me to take Goldie out before I leave?" he offered since it was now dark.

"Thanks but we'll be okay. Goodnight, see you in the morning," she said, climbing down from the cab of his truck. She waved good-bye and went to open the door for Goldie.

After watching Goldie from the porch, she let her back in and locked the door behind her. Standing in the living room, she looked around at the emptiness and remembered how wonderful it felt to have Jack's arm around her shoulders giving her a little hug. Remembering how the touch made her feel brought back memories of Drew like a flood filling her heart as she thought about his touch, his laugh, and the many things that showed he cared. This flood of emotion nearly astounded her. Overwhelmed by uncontrollable sorrow, she ran to her bedroom, threw herself across the bed, and heaved mournful cries that came from deep in her soul.

On awaking the next morning, still in her clothes from the night before, she showered, and then dried her hair and looking in the mirror saw the puffiness under her eyes and in her eyelids. Masking her face with some foundation to cover the signs of her crying binge, she took a long look at her image in the glass in front of her. Giving herself a strong and long talking to, she decided it was past time to move on into the future.

*****

Still feeling the surge of emotion from the mere touch, he tried to put the episode behind him only to return to the moment. Driving toward his cabin, he could not help but relive the scene again. He was as surprised as she was when, without thinking, he had put his arm around her shoulders and pulled her towards him and squeezed her against his own body. They had become closer in the past weeks with working together daily and going to church activities. They were learning a lot about each other and he was confident the day would come when he could share his own grief.

He knew she had mixed feelings about any romantic relationship. However working side-by-side every day brought them closer together, they laughed and even disagreed on some things, they liked the same things but most of all he could not for the life of him take his eyes off her. Occasionally she would catch him staring at her but politely ignore it or perhaps she enjoyed it, he was not sure at this point. He knew that he was ready for a more in-depth relationship and it was getting more difficult to avoid the issue. Perhaps today's lapse of restraint would lead to a deeper awakening and he could proceed with the next step. *What would that be?* He had no clue.

Chapter **6**

Bare tree limbs changed the view around them, as they looked out over the winding road typical of the Ozarks from the windows in the Honeymoon Suite. They removed layer after layer of wallpaper and Krista was replacing it using a faux technique to simulate antique paper with stenciling on the high ceilings and over the window and doorways.

"Jack, do you like to fish?" she called down from her lofty perch on the scaffolding Jack had rigged up for her.

"Yeah, do you?" he asked cutting in with paint around the large windows

"I was thinking, come Saturday, you and I could meet Sandy and her two kids at the cabin. We could pack a picnic and have a little outing. What do you think?" Krista said hoping he would agree.

"That sounds really nice, do you have fishing gear?" he said before thinking.

"Do I have fishing gear? I'll have you know Jack Nolan that I'm the champion when it comes to catching the big ones, you wait and see," Krista said with pride.

"Could I bring my boat?" Jack asked

"You have a boat?" Krista teased.

"Yes, not a big one, it's a flat bottom but it does the job. I bought it from a fellow that came up from Florida where they use them for rescue boats. Can I launch it at your place," he asked.

"You sure can," she said, "the fishing ought to be good about now before the water gets too cold. I'll make a batch of potato salad and some baked beans."

"Do you have a grill? I could grill some steaks," he said.

"Ye of little faith, you don't think we will catch enough fish," she teased.

"Well, just in case you aren't as good as you say you are, I'll bring the steaks and what do you think about asking Bud to come? Do you think Sandy would mind?"

"No that's a great idea."

Plans made, Krista called Sandy. She said they might not get there until mid-morning since her son Brad had a football game on Friday night and would most likely sleep in. However, she thought it sounded like fun and she was anxious to meet Jack.

"Why don't I pick up dessert," Sandy told her

"What, no homemade pie, cake or cookies," Krista challenged her.

"No, just store-bought, but I could stop in Garfield and pick up some of that good ice cream," she said to redeem herself. "Tell me again how to get to the cabin."

Krista gave her directions, then before saying goodbye. She told her friend, "Dress warm, it's starting to get nippy out, especially near the water."

Sandy was somewhat surprised that Krista would take Jack to the cabin, let alone the rest of them. As far as she knew, Krista had not invited anyone to the cabin since Drew's death. Although it was their private world in the woods, they had taken friends and clients there on occasion.

Sandy had a feeling all along that Jack was a special person. Krista had shared with her about the choir director discovery and it seemed as if Jack was feeding her bits and pieces of his history as they grew in their knowledge of each other's past. Sandy had been busy with opening her new agency and running teenagers here and there and had not had an opportunity to go to Eureka Springs. So, she looked forward to this day spent with her good friend.

*****

Bud accepted the invite right away, saying it was his off shift, and getting away for a day would be a good relief, and meeting someone new was always welcome. He sensed that Krista recognized him but knew better than to reveal anything. She would piece it together on her own. He had not even told Jack. He and Jack were best friends and usually shared things, but sometimes feelings, especially raw feelings lie best unsaid. Jack had been through a lot with Debbie. Every time Bud brought someone to the hospital during her illness, Jack was there. Jack and Debbie were the kind of couple you dreamed you would be fortunate enough to be like someday. Bud dated, but nothing became serious. Just about the time, he thought a relationship might go to the next level, leading to marriage, it would fizzle and he would be left scratching his head wondering what he had done wrong. "Maybe you try too hard or you could be picking the wrong ones," Jack told him on an occasion when they talked about women. It was the first time he had admitted he longed for a permanent relationship, one with a wife and kids, the "whole enchilada as they say," he told Jack.

*****

Saturday turned out to have perfect weather, with temperature in the sixties. Jack and Bud had launched the boat and Krista had the fishing gear ready when Sandy arrived with her son and daughter. Krista ran back up the hill to the cabin when she heard the car, to make room for Sandy's dessert in the refrigerator.

"Knock, knock. Anyone at home?" Sandy called out coming through the front door of the cabin.

"In here, hi Brad, Ginny, it's so good to see you again. Brad, you can go down to the dock with the guys if you want to. We girls are going to put some food together."

"Thanks," Brad said with relief.

"I like this cabin," Sandy said looking around.

"Oh, haven't you been here before?" Krista said.

"I don't think so. I would have remembered. Here let me help you with that," Sandy said taking a tray of snacks and following Krista out to the deck.

"I thought this would hold us until dinner."

Soon Brad, Bud, and Jack joined the girls on the deck and Krista introduced everyone. Bud asked Sandy how she and Krista knew each other.

"We worked at the bank together in Rogers," she told him.

"Sandy has started her own business and is now managing the lease on my home in Rogers," Krista said, staring at Bud for recognition.

Molly Owen

"Oh, I didn't know you owned a home in Rogers, I worked for the fire department there until last year," Bud said, trying to jog her memory. "But they had a position open in Eureka and I jumped at the chance to get back closer to my old stomping grounds."

Krista sat still, frozen in time like a stone, he was the paramedic that came to her house when Drew collapsed. *That is where she had seen him before.*

"Krista, are you all right?" Jack said, noticing the look on her face as if she had seen a ghost.

"I'm fine, we need to put these things away if we are going to go fishing," she said, gathering the plates. Sandy reached for the glasses and helped get things back into the kitchen.

"What's wrong?" she quizzed

"I just realized that Bud was the paramedic that came when I called 911 the night Drew died. I knew I had seen him before somewhere."

"Are you alright?"

"Yeah, it just brought back memories, things I had almost forgotten until now."

Back on the deck, "well, now that we've had some fortification maybe we should go catch our supper," Jack said. "Who wants to go fishing?" raising his voice so Krista could hear.

Everyone met on the dock followed by Goldie who instinctively jumped into the boat. After seating instructions, everyone settled into the boat with life jackets and fishing gear, while Jack pushed the boat away from the dock and headed for deeper water. The motor idling so as not to stir up the fish, he slowly maneuvered out into the open water finding a perfect place along the shoreline among the weeds, not far from where they started and dropped anchor.

"This looks like a fishy place, don't you think Krista?" Jack called to her at the front of the boat.

"Looks good to me captain," she turned and grinned at him.

It was not long until hooks baited and lines in the water, red and white bobbers covered the area. They all sat in perfect silence watching ripples the water made as it slapped against the edge of the boat. About an hour later Krista caught the first fish, a one-pound bass, she put it in the basket making sure the lid was tight. Brad caught the next one and soon they had a basket full.

"Looks like we are having fish for dinner instead of steaks," Jack said guiding the boat back into the cove by the cabin being sure not to snag the bottom with the propeller.

The fellows stayed back to clean the fish while the gals went up the hill to the cabin. Ginny stayed out on the deck giving Sandy and Krista time to talk.

"I like Jack, Krista, he sure is good with the kids, I think Ginny has a crush on him," Sandy said smiling.

"Oh Sandy, she is only thirteen," Krista snapped back at Sandy.

"Exactly, don't you remember those crushes we got when we were her age?" Sandy laughed as she teased her. "Anyway, I like him. He's just so laid back and friendly, not uptight."

"Yeah, he's nothing like Drew was and yet he likes the same things. He built his own cabin and he's a great craftsman, like Drew and, look at him, out their cleaning fish. I don't know Sandy, my feelings about him are very confusing. On one hand, I'm his boss and yet we have become friends and it's so easy to talk to him. He's a believer which is very important and we work well together but I guess I'm not ready for anything beyond that yet," Krista confided in her friend. "What do you think about Bud?"

"He's a funny guy isn't he, lots of humor maybe a little too much if you know what I mean?" Sandy said. "He's quite handsome on a movie star level, I guess it's hard to be common when you find yourself, shall we say extraordinary."

Krista laughed at her friend's take on Bud then said, "He isn't anything like Jack but I do like him and he's Jack's very best friend."

"Well, don't wait too long to take a chance on Jack, he's a good catch, actually I'm surprised he isn't married. Has he told you anything about his personal life? You know romance, wife, girlfriend, that kind of thing," Sandy questioned.

"Not a word and I haven't pried; I figure he'll tell me when he's ready," Krista said, wondering again about Jack's past. If he had a girlfriend, he was very private about it and even though he left every day at four o'clock, he never indicated he was in any hurry to be anywhere except his cabin.

Bud kept a watchful eye up the hill hoping Sandy would find her way back down to the dock. "So what do you think of Sandy," he said to Jack.

"She's everything Krista said about her, I like her, how about you?" Jack said while Brad was out of earshot.

"I don't know, maybe a little bit too sophisticated for an old redneck like me. Anyway, she lives in Rogers. I moved back here because this is where I want to be. She has her Real Estate business in Rogers. You know what I mean, Bro?"

"Yeah, but maybe it's time to branch out. You could stand a little polish."

"You think so?" Bud said with a grin.

"It wouldn't hurt to try, you may learn some things about yourself you didn't know before."

"Like why do women find me repulsive?"

"Or why you deliberately make yourself undesirable. Maybe you're afraid of commitment."

"Wow, you sound like that Dr. Phil guy, on TV."

"Just saying…"

*****

After a fun-filled day, they all packed up and headed back to their real lives away from the seclusion of the cabin in the woods. Bud left first using his four-wheel drive to maneuver the hilly terrain. Sandy and Krista hugged each other with plans of getting together again soon. Jack and Krista loaded his truck with Goldie sitting inside in the back seat of the extended cab. Pulling his boat, they brought up the rear of the caravan. When they came to the highway, they waved as each took their own path.

"I like your friend Sandy, Krista, and she has a couple of swell kids," Jack commented as he pulled out onto the highway headed back to Eureka Springs.

"Thank you, they liked you too, as a matter of fact, I think Ginny has a crush on you," Krista teased.

"You don't say, well, she is a cute kid but a little young for this old man." Jack laughed.

Krista loved his sense of humor and the way his face lit up every time he smiled or laughed. Sandy was right, he was a good catch, she just wished she knew more about him and his past.

He left Krista and Goldie at the front door to her living quarters after helping her carry in supplies from the day at the cabin. It did not go unnoticed that she looked especially attractive in her going to the cabin clothes including the oversized flannel shirt and her hair pulled back under a ball cap with her ponytail hanging down above the adjustment strap. She appeared very serious about the great outdoors and proved to adapt to the rigors of the rugged woods and primitive living in the cabin. He saw her daily in her painting work clothes, however, this was different, this was who she was and liked to be and he found it very alluring.

She was complex in her makeup and he felt he had seen all sides of her except the one that would allow him to confide in her and open the door to his soul. He was sure that her feelings were still too raw to accept the tragedy of another right now and therefore he would not reveal anything just yet. Up until now, he had felt like a big brother but that was beginning to change and it scared him, while still bringing on the excitement of the prospect of a new romance in his life for the first time in many years.

*****

Krista watched Jack raking the leaves in and around the flowerbeds, birdbath swing, and old-fashioned metal chairs through the kitchen window. The morning sun shining on his blond hair made it appear two shades lighter. Thoughts of Drew entered uncontrollably, remembering how he loved to clean up the yard around the house in Rogers. He was meticulously neat and the thought of leaves cluttering his lawn was a little beyond his realm of comfort. She waved when Jack caught her watching him giving her a big grin that covered most of his face and sent an unusual tingle down her spine. *What was that?* It was hard for her to let natural things, which happened when she was around Jack, go unnoticed but she did wish it would stop. Not sure she was ready for the next level of their relationship, she avoided anything resembling intimacy, almost to the point of downright rudeness, and then would regret her actions. Why can't things just stay as they are for a while? She would ask herself, however she knew the answer to that question and it put fear in her, a fear of what, she was not quite sure of, yet. So, she bowed her head and talked to her heavenly Father asking his will to be done in matters of her heart. *Heavenly Father, help me clear my head of fear of the unknown. Give me clarity on where my relationship with Jack is concerned. Lord help me live in the present and accept your will. These things I ask in Jesus' name. Amen.*

Chapter 7

Work on the Inn was nearly finished after weeks of stripping wallpaper, painting, refinishing floors, and deep cleaning. Krista selected red paint for the exterior of the building and decided to name the bed and breakfast: The Red Lady Inn. She saved the living quarters until later figuring they could always work on it while renting rooms in the Inn. Now it was time to tackle the gift shop with new fixtures and a more romantic look for the vintage ware and apparel Krista planned to feature. After many meetings with vendors, she formulated a design for the new shop she planned to name after her mother, Victoria. She hired a young designer, Sarah, from church that would help her put together the display windows. She wanted to have a grand opening for the Christmas holiday season when Eureka Springs opened the town for one last retail blow out before closing for the winter.

Molly Owen

"Do you have plans for Thanksgiving?" Krista asked.

"Well, I'll probably go to Berryville," Jack answered from the ladder where he worked on the medallion he was putting above the antique light fixtures that hung over the glass counters where the jewelry would be displayed.

"Do you have family there?" she asked curiously.

"I have a sister with her family and some friends," he told her. "What about you? Where are you spending Thanksgiving?"

"I think I'll spend it with Sandy in the cabin. Her kids will be with their Dad." She said.

"I see," he said remembering that Krista's family was gone, so the best friends would spend that time together as it should be for both of them.

"Jack, tell me about your family."

"Not much to tell, Dad died when I was a teenager and Mom died a few years ago. She never remarried, said God gave her the love of her life and she felt blessed by that. I have a brother, somewhere, we haven't seen or heard from him in years and then my baby sister who is married with three young kids. Oh, my aunt lives there, my mother's sister and I guess that's it," he said matter of fact.

Krista thought about what he said about his mother not remarrying and wondered if it was the way she felt about Drew. She loved him very much and they had a good marriage, however, there was always something missing. Drew did not want any children and that was hard for Krista to accept. They discussed it once or twice but then the subject did not come up again because each time it ended in a huge argument. She always wanted a big family since she was an only child and was very much aware of the limited time she had left to give birth to children.

"Penny for your thoughts, as they say," Jack said, climbing down from the ceiling folding the ladder and leaning it against the wall.

"Just thinking about what your mother said about not remarrying," Krista replied.

"What makes you think about that?" Jack said coming over to the window where Krista handed Jack the step stool.

"I'm not sure I feel that way about my marriage, not that it wasn't good. But, I think if the right man came along I would remarry," she said casually not thinking how it may sound.

"I know what you mean, Krista, I was married before. I haven't wanted to burden you with this until I felt you were ready," he said and continued to tell her the story of his short marriage to Debbie. "I loved her very deeply, we were high school sweethearts. The friends I told you about in Berryville, well, they are Debbie's parents and I spend part of the holidays with them just like we did before Debbie died."

"Now I know why you understand, you have been there and know what I'm going through. I'm so sorry Jack and I want you to know how much I appreciate you being there for me during my grieving. It must have been very hard for you." Krista said looking deep into his eyes.

"There were times when I was not sure I would make it, but I had my work with the cabin I was building and the church that kept me going. This community became my family and the church my home," he explained. "We waited to get married until I got out of college. Sometimes I look back and wonder why we waited, we could have had more time together. I wish we had gotten married right out of high school, but then I remember how wonderful it was for the first couple of years after the wedding and I thank God for that time."

They sat next to each other on the wood floor leaning back against the wooden counter for a long while, there in the dim light of the gift shop, as they shared their feelings and learned more about one another. The sun was down early and dense dark shadows from the building covered the street as one after another light flickered in the windows across the street and up the hill. Silence filled the warm room as each fell into their own thoughts. Jack stood up and reached down for Krista's hand. As he pulled her to her feet, he leaned down and kissed her forehead.

"I better get out of here, I have a project that needs to be finished before winter sets in and it gets dark so early I have to use floodlights," he said.

"Jack?"

"Yes."

"Thank you."

"What for?"

"Everything," she said heading for the stairs.

"I'll walk up with you after I lock up down here. I'm parked on the upper road."

She walked him through her apartment and watched as he drove down the street. The kiss was sweet and tender, not at all what she expected for a first kiss, and yet it astounded her. Her head told her she was not ready but her heart begged for this relationship. She missed being touched, loved, held, and yes, kissed. She told herself that she was still young with a lifetime ahead of her and was it wrong to want to be happy in a romantic loving relationship. Falling in love again was the furthest thing from her mind over the past few months. But, now she looked at her future and felt the longing for companionship. *Dear Father, if this is Your will and You bless a relationship between me and Jack, then please help me to take one step at a time until I'm sure. Thank You in Your Son's name. Amen.*

*****

Jack hoped he had not pushed things with Krista, however, he was becoming more attracted to her as time went on and perhaps now was the time to let her know his feelings. Sharing his grief with her was the right thing to do and he was sure the timing was right and that she could handle it. She had not drowned him in questions but accepted the things he told her. He was sure she wanted more information but like her, he planned to give it to her one piece at a time. Listening to her story gave him an insight into who she was and he wanted her to have the same insight about him. He wanted her to know him with all the good and the bad. So, he was sure the questions would come, and now he was ready to share his past with her.

Driving onto the road that led to his hideaway, he decided to pursue a relationship with Krista, in the hope that it would lead them to a future together. He was pleased that she was a committed Christian because any girl he became serious about would have to be a believer.

The headlights of his pickup showed on the cabin just as he saw a shadow run out the back door. Pressing the accelerator, he sped up throwing rocks behind the truck as the tires churned and skidded on the driveway. He saw the figure run through the creek bed and into the dense woods behind the shed at the back of the property. He grabbed the flashlight out of the glove compartment and leaving the truck ran toward the area where he saw someone go through the trees. With his long stride, he walked over the trickle of water flowing in the bottom of the creek. He shined the light back and forth in the dark without a sign of anyone hiding. Eventually, he returned to the cabin to find nothing out of place. *Strange,* he thought, *maybe I caught him in the act before he had a chance to take anything, I better check the shed where the tools are,* he thought, going out the screen door and back out to the shed. Unlocking the door, he looked around and took a quick inventory of the contents discovering that nothing was missing. Then remembering to lock the door again thought *the door WAS locked.*

Back in the kitchen, he discovered missing food, and a couple of sodas gone from the refrigerator. *The fellow must be on the run to steal something to eat*, he thought, putting his own dinner on the table. He reminded himself to lock up tighter when he left for Berryville in a few days.

*****

"Once in a while, a raccoon manages to invade my screened-in porch, they make mincemeat out of screen wire if they think there is something to eat, but I have never had a human intruder before. He's probably moved on, just a drifter. He had better find a place to stay pretty quick before winter sets in." Jack told Krista while they cleaned up the mess left from yesterday's projects.

"Be real careful Jack, he could be dangerous. Drew worried about someone breaking into our cabin and he didn't like me to go out there by myself, but I always feel safe because it is so isolated you need a map to find it." Krista said.

"I think Drew was right, you shouldn't be out there by yourself. If, by no other way, someone could find you by water just by taking their boat up to your cove. And, you said yourself there are hunters in the area. No, you need to be really careful when you're alone at your cabin." Jack said with urgency.

"Well, Jack Nolan, I think you care," she teased.

"You know I care, so don't take this lightly, miss independence, this could be serious, so promise me you'll not go out there alone. Maybe it's not such a good idea for you and Sandy to go there for Thanksgiving because of all the hunting. Why don't you invite Sandy over here? She hasn't seen your place, yet." Jack encouraged her.

"That's a great idea, Jack, that would be fun and Sandy could have one of the new or should I say old rooms in the Inn. She would like that. Thanks for the suggestion and know this Mr. Nolan, I'm not doing this because you don't want us at the cabin by ourselves," she winked at him.

"Right, I know you won't do anything against my wishes though, will you?" he looked at her pleading. "I admit this incident at my place has me a little on guard and you should be too. I'll take your advice about being careful because he could be dangerous and you take my advice because it could be dangerous for you."

*****

Krista opened Victoria's for the first time the day before Thanksgiving and Sandy promised to help out in the shop for the next few days. The day had a steady flow of visitors, mostly lookers, but sales were more than Krista expected. She handed out flyers announcing the opening and as people came into the shop, she gave them brochures of The Red Lady Inn that had reservation information and the dates of the grand opening. All and all it was a very successful day, and Krista was encouraged by several favorable comments.

That evening Sandy arrived with a boxed store-bought pizza and colas for their pre-thanksgiving dinner. "You can't beat Walmart's pizza. We have them all the time," Sandy told Krista.

"Did you have any trouble finding me?"

"No, it's been so long since I've been in Eureka Springs that I couldn't help but look around at the changes."

"I know, it was kind of a diamond in the rough for a while and now it has flourished into a wonderful tourist attraction again," Krista said, putting the pizza in the oven.

"I like your place, it's cozy and yet very roomy."

"Thanks, we are almost ready to start the remodel up here. I still have some decisions to make but once we get started I think it will go pretty fast and then it will feel more like me, like home."

"I can't wait to see the rest of the Inn and what you've done," Sandy said.

When they finished eating Krista took her friend on a tour of the Inn starting at the top and ending in the shop.

Molly Owen

"Oh, Krista, it's beautiful, I can't believe you and Jack have done all this work and I had no idea you were a decorator, I thought your house in Rogers was neat but this is magnificent, full of charm and history," Sandy said while going from room to room. "And this gift shop, what a wonderful idea, I'm sure it will go over big, especially here in this turn of the century town, it just fits like a glove."

"It has been fun, a lot of work, but fun. I've done lots of research discovering the décor of that era and of course I've had much help from the historical society and the owners association," Krista said with pride. "Remember all the magazine clippings I've saved over the years, will it comes in handy during this process and the best part is Jack goes along with everything I suggest. He tells me if it's possible and then we dig in. I couldn't have accomplished all of this without him."

"How is Jack?" Sandy asked curiously to know if there were sparks between them.

"Oh he's great; he went to Berryville for Thanksgiving with his family," Krista told Sandy as they made their way back upstairs. "I have a better idea of who he is since he told me about his wife Debbie. At least Drew went fast and I didn't have to watch him die a slow death as Jack did with Debbie. I think that would be awful."

"Has he had any more uninvited guests at his place?" Sandy asked as they settled on the couch with a fresh cup of coffee.

"Not that he has told me, and I 'm sure he would tell me since now he's concerned about my safety. I just never think about things like that but I guess men like protecting their women." Krista commented. "What?" she said looking at Sandy's grin?

"I was just wondering if Jack worries about your safety because he considers you his woman," Sandy teased her friend.

Ignoring her comment she continued to lead Sandy up the stairs. Then stopping she opened the door to the honeymoon suite. Retrieving her things from the living quarters, Krista took Sandy's suitcase to the trunk at the end of the bed. "Here is your luxury plus, have a good night's rest and I'll see you in the morning at breakfast," she said leaving the room.

"It's absolutely charming, I love it," Sandy called after Krista who by this time was entering her own quarters.

The Jacuzzi was enticing, and Sandy could not wait to get in. Testing the temperature, she climbed into the warm water. With her head resting on the side, she melted under the swirl of the bubbles. *What a wonderful place to be, I needed this, and a perfect time too with the kids at their Dad's.* She told herself closing her eyes and relaxing letting all thoughts disappear into the night.

*****

Krista rose early from the night's rest to put the small turkey in the oven, and then she made a pot of coffee. The aroma from the coffee woke Sandy from one of the best nights of sleep she had had in a long while. She made her bed putting everything back just like it was and surveying the room she followed the call of a hot cup of java. Upstairs, she found Krista in her kitchen putting on the final touches of their Thanksgiving meal.

"Good morning, did you sleep well?" Krista asked.

"Like a baby. It was wonderful waking up in that gorgeous room, I feel like a special person," Sandy told her friend.

"You are a very special friend and you deserve a vacation from the daily grind of life, we all do, don't you think? That's why places like this are so popular, it's a place away from everything, no responsibilities, no deadlines, just relaxation." Krista said pouring hot coffee into the cup Sandy held out for her.

"I'm sold," she said, taking a sip of coffee. Anxious to work in the shop downstairs she asked, "Yummy, what brand is this?"

"It's a special blend I'll be selling."

"Very tasty, kind of a nutty flavor, I like it. What time do we open the shop?'

"About 10 o'clock. I have the turkey on low so it will be ready about the time we close around four," Krista told her

They had picked out their vintage outfits to wear as shopkeepers the night before and after breakfast; they put on their attires, feeling like they had walked out of the pages of *Little Women*. Krista took Sandy's hand bowing their heads. She said a prayer. *"Father, thank you for this friendship and for bringing Sandy here safely and thank you for our time together. I pray that we make our customers feel at home and that they leave our store having a good experience. Please be with Sandy's kids and with Jack and his family. I pray this in Jesus' name. Amen."* Then they descended the stairs to the shop.

The day saw a steady flow of people, most of whom were curious to see the new shop in town, but to Krista's delight, some actually made purchases making the day a profitable one. Four o'clock came and, as usual, darkness set in early with street lights illuminating the area. As Krista locked the front glass door she noticed someone in the shadow of the building across the street. Carefully taking the string covered ring, she pulled the old-fashioned shade down over the door and turned on the neon-lit "closed" sign before pulling the curtains behind the display windows.

The two women finished putting things away, swept the floor, counted the receipts for the day, turned out the lights, and headed up the stairs. Krista stopped on the second floor and with the excuse of checking on the ceiling fans, she sent Sandy ahead to change her clothes and told her she would meet her in her quarters. The room that faced the front of the Inn was dark as she went to pull the shade away from the window just enough to see that the figure had moved out of the shadows toward the Inn. She watched as the tall, thin man crossed the street then moved to another window. She saw him with his hands in his pockets and head hung low as he walked slowly toward Spring Street.

It would have never occurred to her to be concerned if Jack had not had his uninvited visitor, then again, for some reason, she found herself more curious than afraid. Although not expecting any problems she thought it wise to inform Sandy of what she had observed since four eyes were better than two and they could keep a watch out for anything unusual.

After changing her own clothes, she found Sandy sitting in the living room. "It sure smells good in here. Too bad the Schmidts couldn't come, they went to Texas to be with their daughter. I don't know about you but I love turkey leftovers," Krista said, taking the bird out of the oven.

"Oh, me too, there is nothing like a roasted turkey sandwich," Sandy said, putting plates and silverware on the counter. "I guess Bud decided not to come?"

"He's working a four-day shift, actually he's fixing the firehouse thanksgiving dinner, he said, with all the trimmings."

"A man that cooks…that's interesting."

"I thought you didn't care for his style."

"But Krista…he cooks…."

They both laughed until their sides ached and tears rolled down their faces.

"So do you know how to carve a turkey?" Krista asked her friend.

"Not really. I have tried a couple of times but it never looks like when the ex carved it. I'm willing to try if you trust me with that beautiful bird. It looks too good to put a carving knife to it." Sandy said, looking at Krista for approval.

With a plate of dark and light turkey meat on a platter and the rest of the Thanksgiving dishes including Krista's famous dressing on the counter, Krista told Sandy to help herself.

During dinner, Krista told Sandy about the person she saw across the street. "Do you think it could be the same guy that Jack saw the other night?"

"I don't know but we will need to be more aware of our surroundings," Krista said clearing the table and putting away the food. As Sandy helped dry the dishes, they agreed to be careful, and then turned in for the night in order to be up early in the morning to be shopkeepers again.

At sunrise, they once again dressed in their vintage attire and went downstairs to open the shop. Krista raised the shade on the front door; subconsciously searching the area with her eyes for anything out of the ordinary before unlocking the door. Seeing nothing, she soon forgot the incident while serving her many customers. The day was very busy with intermittent lulls as they worked together just as they had at the bank in Rogers.

At the end of the day, they ate a light supper of leftovers and relaxed for some real girl talk. "How do you like living in Eureka Springs?" Sandy asked.

"I find the people here are very friendly and helpful, especially the people I've met through the church. I like singing in the choir and I feel a spiritual enrichment after each Sunday's service." Krista said.

Sandy had waited to ask the question she had wanted to ask ever since she arrived. "What is happening between you and Jack?"

"I do like him and we have become good friends," Krista said.

"But?"

"I don't know Sandy. After Harold left you, did you want another man or did you just want what you had, you know with him?" Krista questioned.

"I guess I went through all the stages of grieving as you have. A divorce is like a death, the death of a marriage, I think the difference is you feel rejected, unworthy, useless and there is as in my case a lot of anger, bitterness even hatred." Sandy told her. "In answer to your question, yes, I wanted things to be like they were. I was very much in love with Harold and it hurt deep inside to discover his love for me was not sincere and that he could even think of someone other than me to live with and sleep with and spend the rest of his life with the person he met and had an affair with on a whim. I became a very bitter person and the idea of loving another man was far from my thoughts for the future, however, I missed the intimacy of a marital relationship, you know, private jokes winking across the room and a connection with someone who knows you better than anyone. We were married for twelve years. Then there is always the fear of another failed marriage."

"I know there are not many men in your life now, but did you date?" Krista asked

"Not much, I just couldn't. I have two kids and their future to think about and for that matter my own future to plan. Maybe when the kids are grown, I'll get into the dating game but right now I have too much on my plate to complicate it with figuring out the wants, desires, and expectations of a man." Sandy said a little surprised at her reaction to Krista's question. "I did have a close call a few years back, but it wasn't meant to be and I just couldn't bring myself to committing to something that wasn't right for me. The kids loved him, he was a teacher at Brad's school, I broke it off when I realized I felt desperate for the affection of a male but I didn't love him."

"Drew wasn't a perfect man and we had one major disagreement about having kids. I guess I never told you about that. At times, our lives were so full it didn't seem to matter but then I would feel that tug in my heart. I love kids and I always imagined having a big family. I guess that was because I was an only child. However, like you, I loved Drew and I know he loved me just as much and even without having children, we had a good marriage. I don't like comparing Jack to Drew but I can't seem to keep from it," Krista said. "Sometimes I lie awake at night and wonder if I'll ever have the same closeness, intimacy, with another man. I want to marry again. I think I am too young to go through life without a mate and maybe, who knows, I could have that family I always wanted. Do you ever ask what God wants for you?"

"I do, but I have a bad habit of not listening to Him or I should say not hearing Him. What do you think God wants for you?" Sandy said.

"After Drew died, I seriously thought about going into missionary work in some foreign country but that is not where God was leading me and I think for whatever reason he led me to this Inn. From the time I read the ad in the paper, I was headed full steam ahead to this place and I have never looked back or regretted my decision. I'm not sure what else He has in store for me, but my prayer is that His will, will be done and I believe with all my being that as long as He's in my heart, my life will be wonderful." Krista confides in Sandy.

"I have always admired your faith and your positive outlook on life, Krista; you're a real inspiration to me. I believe in God and His Son and I try to follow His teachings but somewhere I get a little lost. You have Him walking right beside you all the time. I'm not sure I do. What is the secret?" Sandy questions her younger wiser friend.

"I think having Him in my life means He's there whenever I need to talk, ask questions, thank Him, praise Him, be oh so grateful for His grace. He has not spared me pain in my life but He is always there to see me through. I feel His presence in everything I do. He just makes it easier to take this journey we call life." Krista says with a soft smile on her face. "I just let Him in to be my friend and companion. I'm not perfect, I make mistakes all the time Sandy and sometimes I forget to say I'm sorry or ask for forgiveness but I just keep trying."

With that said, she asked Sandy to pray with her. *"Heavenly Father, thank you for this friendship between two women traveling new pathways in their lives. You are the force that inspires us and protects us, Father. We thank you for your grace and the blessings you give us daily. We pray for everyone's safety while spending this time of Thanksgiving with families and friends. We pray in Jesus' Name. Amen."* After the Amen, they gave each other a big hug and said goodnight.

*****

Jack sat in his truck, the motor still running, looking at the two-story house they lived in after their marriage. The blue shutters on either side of their upstairs bedroom window shown with fresh paint and the lawn below were full of debris from the tall pines that filled the landscape. Debbie loved the sound the pine trees made as they blew in the wind. She would gather pine cones every year and make wreaths to sell at the church bazaar. With a smile on his face, he remembered the turkeys she made out of pine cones and used them for place cards the year they had the two families for Thanksgiving at their house. He could hear her laughter; smell her heavenly scent as if she were sitting beside him. Putting the truck in gear, he drove a few blocks to the cemetery.

Standing in the leaves gathered around his feet, he let the wind blow through his hair. So many memories filled his mind bringing images of Debbie as a young girl in high school with long blonde hair, bright blue eyes, skin like velvet, and a sweet smile that engraved forever on his heart and filled his dreams. If he listened closely, he could hear her voice, soft and tender, telling him of her thoughts and visions for the future. Jack and Debbie, the couple everyone knew would wed someday, raise a family, girls that were as pretty as Debbie was, and boys that looked like Jack.

Looking down just as a gust of wind swept over the stone removing leaves that partially covered the letters, he read her name, Debra Elizabeth Noland. He went to his knees as tears filled the bowls of his eyelids pushing to escape. As if she was there, he felt peace, an acceptance that he longed for. He wanted Debbie's blessing, he wanted her to know how much he loved Krista but at the same time how much he had loved her. Prayer was a part of his daily life and now he wanted Debbie to hear his prayer hopefully for her to pray with him. *"Father, I praise your name, you know my heart, Jesus, I thank you for the blessing of time spent with Debbie and the love that we shared. I didn't think I could ever love someone else and now I find myself in love with Krista. I know in my heart that this is right and I thank you for yet another chance at happiness. Oh, God, thank you for Krista. I so want to take her for my wife. I ask your blessing on this union if she will say yes. In Your Name precious Jesus. Amen.*"

Taking one final look at the stone, he laid his hand on her name, then turned and walked away. A peace surrounded him as he got back in his truck. He sat for a moment, letting this feeling surround him. Turning the key, he put the shift in gear and slowly followed the road out of the cemetery.

Chapter 8

Eureka Springs was dressed for Christmas with green boughs of cedar needles, red bows, angels with wings made of real feathers, and flickering strings of colored lights. The aroma of smoke billowing from the chimneys filled the winter nights and the silence of the white snow covered the sky as it drifted through the alleys and onto the walkways. Hot chocolate and apple cider replaced lemonade and iced tea. Parkas, knit hats, and gloves came out of storage and flannel-lined boots replaced sandals as the snowflakes accumulated into drifts that masked sidewalks and streets. The village nestled in and among the hills of the Arkansas Ozark Mountains became a wonderland reminiscent of the miniature village on display in the shop window downtown.

Molly Owen

Krista gazed out the window of her bedroom at the radiant splendor on the horizon and flashes of memories surrounded her. It was as if she had gone back in time and a feeling of peace engulfed her and put a smile on her face while she prepared for the complexity of winter in Eureka Springs. Startled by the sound of running water somewhere in the Inn, she came back to the present only to realize that Jack stayed in the Inn because of the predicted snowstorm. Hurrying, she got dressed and went to the kitchen to start the coffee. She was not sure whether to call him for breakfast or wait for his arrival on the third floor as she placed several pieces of bacon in the skillet.

"My, that bacon smells good, and I'm starving. Can I help with anything?"

"You could pop some bread slices into the toaster."

"Consider it done. Did you see the snowdrifts outside? It is a good thing I stayed in. It could be days before I get out of here," he said.

"Well, someone told me a long time before winter set in that I should stock up and I took that advice, so we will not starve."

Jack had taken up the carpet, refinished floors in Krista's living area, and now was ready to replace the furniture they had stored in the hallways of the Inn. He winterized his cabin and the weekend before he went with Krista to help her winterize her cabin. The decision to stay at the Inn came when the forecast for the next few days was over a foot of snow. Jack told Krista the old building could rebel against the elements and something could go wrong. Krista was glad to have him stay remembering some of the stories Mrs. Schmidt had told her about winters in the "ole Lady" as she referred to the Inn.

The Schmidts had gone south for the winter. "We are just like the geese, we know when to leave," Mrs. Schmidt had told Krista the Sunday before the big storm.

"I'll surely miss you, but you must promise to call me now and then to let me know how you are," Krista had told them.

"Don't you fret any now, Jack will take good care of you and don't hesitate to ask him for help if you need it," she had told Krista.

Sarah, from church, was working full time in Victoria's and Krista told her they would close the shop during the bad weather and for her not to come in until the roads were passable again.

She set the plate of bacon and eggs in front of him, poured herself another cup of coffee, and sitting down she realized how natural it seemed to be eating breakfast with him. Occasionally he would bring donuts to share in the morning when he arrived for the day. However, this was different. He arrived for work from a room in the Inn downstairs much earlier than before and they were sitting at the counter together in her kitchen eating a big breakfast he had helped her prepare. He reached for her hand across the table and said a short prayer thanking God for His blessings and for the food. Just as they said, "Amen," there was a loud sound like thunder, but closer. Krista jumped and Jack looked out the window just in time to see a large tree crash to the ground missing Krista's car by inches but putting a limb through the roof on her front porch.

"Stay here, I'll go check the damage," he told her.

Shaking off the snow that was still falling, he came back to the kitchen. "Well, we have some major damage to the garden, birdbaths, the gazebo is destroyed so is the fence but the good news is that your car and my pickup are okay and the hole in the porch roof can be repaired easily enough. Another plus, the redbuds and dogwoods are still standing."

"Oh, Jack, I'm so glad you're here. And thank the Lord it didn't crash in here on top of us," she told him.

"Yes, that is a huge oak, but look on the bright side it will make good firewood," he said smiling.

His positive outlook was always a blessing to her, as they had faced many obstacles in the renovation from plumbing to electrical and now falling trees. She would have never thought that a tree would fall and do so much damage. She had put the garden renovation in the March schedule but the budget for the project would not nearly cover the expense of the damage done by the tree. She hoped the insurance would help defray the cost.

Breakfast dishes cleared, they struggled to replace the furniture in the living room, tugging and pulling around tight corners all the while being careful not to fall through the banisters of the stairs and railings along the hallways. Krista had ordered the appliances for her new kitchen and they had put them downstairs in the back of the shop hidden behind screens until the kitchen was redone. The plan was to load them into Jack's pickup drive around to the road above and place them in the kitchen. So they decided to begin demolition of the kitchen in a few days, which would allow time for the snow to melt.

"So you never told me about the girl's weekend, did you two have a good time?"

"Yes, actually it was a wonderful weekend, we bonded and had fun staying up late with lots of girl talk and working with Sandy in the shop was fun. We've always been good friends, but I think we are even better friends now. She confided in me things I never knew before and we have been close for several years. I admire her raising two kids, having a business, mortgage, and all the responsibility of parenting on a daily basis. That must be extremely hard. No wonder she doesn't have time for a man in her life."

"I think Bud liked her, but even though he liked her kids I don't think he's ready for a readymade family. She is doing a good job with her kids. They are both sensible, polite, fun people to be around and I would hope I could be that kind of parent."

"Did you and Debbie want children?"

"Yes, but by the time we were ready to take that step she was diagnosed with cancer and it was totally out of the picture. I enjoy being with my sister's kids. They are great kids and my time with them is way too short. How about you?"

"What do you mean?"

"Did you and Drew plan to have children?"

"That was one thing we never agreed on. I wanted a large family and Drew thought to have each other should be enough. He never wanted to have children."

"That must have been hard for you," Jack said wondering how one goes about not having children in a loving marriage if they are able, except perhaps in the case of genetics passed down through generations causing issues with the child's health. Or in his and Debbie's case issues for the mother.

"It was, I thought after Drew died that if we had had children I would still have a part of him with me. I never understood his not wanting children and now I sometimes wonder if he was being selfish. He went so far as to make sure we didn't have children. I didn't know he was going to have a vasectomy," she said and as an afterthought said, "I'm glad *I* can still have children."

"Maybe he was afraid of you being pregnant," Jack said, taking note of her comment about being able to have children.

"I never thought of that, he did have a sister who died in childbirth, she was several years older than Drew. Jack, you are so perceptive. I would rather think that he was afraid for me to be pregnant than remember him being selfish."

The grin that covered his face always put Krista at ease and this time she studied his face as he told her that every experience in life brings a new perspective, a new priority, a new outlook, or an understanding of situations. He told her of his commitment to be aware of people and understand the burdens they may be carrying unknown to anyone around them.

"After Debbie died, I was walking dead myself and the people around me had no idea the burden I carried. This made me realize how I didn't know the burden other people carried and I decided to be more aware, and kinder to the world around me. It was my gift to Debbie's memory," he said.

"Jack, that is beautiful. What a wonderful way to remember her, so every time you take the time to understand a situation you're honoring her memory," she said with a tear running down her face. "You were deeply in love."

*****

The storm that put a blanket of white on the Ozarks had moved on and warm weather came on its heels melting the snow and allowing the tree removal that made enough firewood for two winters. Christmas day was fast approaching and all the shops in town were open for business. In spite of the buzzing chainsaw, cutting up the fallen tree, the shop stayed open and sales increased. The business association planned a Christmas party and Jack invited Krista to be his date. Everyone was to dress in vintage attire for an old fashioned Christmas gala.

The night of the event Jack planned a surprise he hoped would knock her off her feet. Krista had a few plans of her own to impress Jack with slenderizing floor-length heirloom silk and lace gown in a champagne color with lace bolero that covered the ivory skin tones of her bare shoulders. She pulled her short red hair back and attached clipped earrings with jewels that matched the buckle on the sash at the waist of the dress to her tiny ears that completed the outfit. Her brown high-top, lace-up shoes finished the vintage look. Several women in town bought their dresses for the event at Krista's shop and she was especially careful not to wear anything that others may be wearing. Looking in the full-length mirror, she turned from one side to the other and finally approved her image.

The knock at her door brought her excitement and anticipation as she took her cream velvet cape from the hook and awaited the surprise Jack had promised. When she opened the door, Jack grinned from ear to ear, "you're beautiful," he said then stepping aside he gestured toward the white horse and buggy that sat majestically on the street. "Oh, Jack how wonderful," she said.

Jack in his black tails and tie held his hand out and taking her hand he placed it on his arm as he escorted her to the awaiting carriage. He carefully helped her climb the steps and waited until she was in the buggy seat then went back and locked the door.

Goldie whined and Jack told her they would be back soon. Returning to the buggy, he took his place beside Krista and pulled the blanket up over their laps. The crisp night air caused puffs of moisture to form with each breath. They rode to the Center under the streetlights just as it would have been a century ago. Jack put his arm around her shoulders and pulled her close to him to keep her warm. She smiled at his romantic gesture as the horse clip-clopped along the concrete streets.

On their arrival, Jack helped her down from the buggy then escorted her inside where the party was in full swing with decorations that Krista helped put together. He took her cape and old-fashioned fur muffler that kept her hands warm and they found a spot. Guests surrounded the refreshment table, filled with apple cider, truffles, petite cakes, and winter fruits. Jack brought Krista a cup of apple cider, handing it to her with a wink and smile, then sitting next to her at the table he found it hard to take his eyes off her.

"You look radiant tonight Krista, that dress is perfect for you," he said almost in a whisper.

"Thank you, Jack, I'm glad you like it, it's one of my favorites."

Soon the band played a waltz and Jack asked Krista to dance. She was amazed at how gracefully he led her around the floor. She didn't notice the floor clearing of other couples until the end of the dance when everyone clapped. Still holding her hand, he stepped back and bowed while she curtsied. They both laughed and hurried back to their table.

"Jack, you're a fantastic dancer, smooth as silk and where did you learn to waltz?" Krista said breathlessly.

"Would you believe that I took ballroom dancing?"

"I would believe it after dancing with you but if you had told me before I would have probably laughed."

"It takes a good dance partner to make a guy look good and Krista you have danced a few steps in your time."

"I too took ballroom dancing while in high school. I love to dance and you're right, it helps to have a good partner."

"Well, we are finding out more and more things that make us good partners, shall we do it again?" he winked at her as he led her back on the dance floor.

She felt like a princess with her prince at the royal ball. He was so attentive, never leaving her side, and every time he winked at her, she felt her knees weaken. He was so handsome and carried himself tall and proud next to her petite stature yet she felt comfortable as they glided around the floor under the many-colored lights cast on the dancers from the large disco ball hanging above them. She closed her eyes and enjoyed the moment. Meanwhile, Jack smiled as her red hair shone like a beacon among the others dancing around them.

They mingled with the other business owners and compared notes on keeping the shops open during the holidays. The evening was ending as they announced the last dance. It was a slow dance to one of Ann Murray's recordings. As the words, *Could I have this dance for the rest of my life?*, filled the room Jack pulled her close to him, she closed her eyes and they danced effortlessly then Krista felt Jack kiss her on top of her head. She raised her face to his and stopping in the middle of the dance floor, he leaned down and kissed her. She felt her legs go limp then the music stopped and the lights came on leaving them standing still arm in arm. Slowly they walked hand in hand back to the table to gather Krista's clutch purse and gloves.

Leaving the building, several people told them good-bye, and some remarked at what a handsome couple they made. As preplanned, the horse and carriage went back to the stable during the dance. Jack left his pickup earlier so they could ride with a heater as the temperature began to drop. They walked the short distance to the truck and he helped her up onto the running board and made sure her dress gathered inside the cab before shutting the door. They sat in the parking lot under a light on top of a pole casting white beams through the windshield, waiting for the heater to warm up. Silence, except for the motor running finally broke when Krista told Jack she had a wonderful time and everything was perfect. Jack turned facing her and taking in a deep breath told her.

"Krista, I can't begin to tell you what a difference you have made in my life. Since the first day I met you, I have felt close to you. We've become friends and now I'm in love with you," as Krista started to say something he put his finger to her mouth and continued. "We have both had major losses in our life but we are young and we could build a lifetime together, I just hope you feel the same way I do."

"I do Jack, and after tonight I have no doubts," Krista answered and leaned over for another kiss. "I'm in love with you Jack and I'm convinced we are meant to be together."

"Krista Moore, will you marry me?" Jack said looking into her eyes.

"Yes, Jack Nolan, I'll marry you," Krista answered and waited for Jack's smile that she loved so much. "I do have one question, where will we live?"

Jack laughed, "Well, we certainly have some choices, don't we? I love you Krista and wherever we live, I know we will be happy. I just want to hold you forever," he said, putting his arms around her giving her a bear hug.

"Jack, remember the morning you helped me make breakfast? Well, I knew then that we were going to be fine together. I have loved you from the start, I just felt guilty because of Drew and I didn't know if you could love me because of your deep love for Debbie. However, as time has gone by I have waited for you to tell me how you felt," Krista shared.

They were the only ones left in the parking lot and the windows fogged from the heater. One last kiss and Jack took

Krista home. He helped her down from the truck and walked her down the sidewalk. Leaving her at her door after one more kiss, he left with the promise of being there early in the morning to take her to Church.

Krista could not wait to call Sandy and tell her about her fairy tale evening. Even at this late hour, she knew her friend would understand. She dialed the number and let it ring several times. Then she hung up thinking that in her excitement she had dialed the wrong number. She dialed again, this time becoming concerned. She called Sandy's cell phone, it rang four times before Sandy answered.

"Hello," Sandy's voice answered with a strain.

"Sandy, it's me, I'm sorry to call so late but I have wonderful news, did I wake you?" Krista said, excited to hear Sandy's voice.

"No, I'm at the hospital, Brad was hurt at the football game tonight," Sandy said.

"Oh Sandy, is he alright?" Krista said, forgetting all about her wonderful news.

"I don't know yet, they are running tests, Krista I'm so scared, he could be paralyzed. It's his neck," Sandy began to cry.

"Where are you?"

"Rogers," Sandy answered.

Molly Owen

"We're coming. Don't worry we'll be there soon." Krista said.

She hung up the phone and ran to change clothes then she called Jack. After telling him about Brad, they decided that she would drive out to his place and they would go from there. She had never been to his place but was sure she could find it. She ran out to her car, unlocked the door, and started the motor. When she turned on the lights, she saw what she thought was a man running down the street. *How odd,* she thought, *What is he doing out here in the cold at this time of night?* She asked herself as she pulled out onto the street. She passed him on the road and if she had not been in such a hurry, she would probably have stopped.

Pulling into the driveway, she parked next to Jack's truck. He came out and told her they should take his truck since it had four-wheel drive if they ran into ice or snow. She climbed into the cab where she was just minutes ago, happy, unconcerned and now the mood was very different as she told Jack everything she knew.

"Oh and the strangest thing when I pulled out of the parking space a man was running down the street, at this time of night in the cold."

"Maybe the guy had been to a social event with his girlfriend and was running to stay warm on his way home," Jack said, trying not to sound alarmed.

Satisfied with the scenario Jack presented she put it out of her mind and concentrated on the trip ahead to the hospital to be with Sandy.

Maneuvering the dangerous curves and hills of the Ozarks especially in the dense darkness of the winter night was a challenge for the best of drivers. The heavy moisture hanging in the air began to form into ice crystals. First it was light and airy then they heard the sleet as it hit the metal and glass on the truck. Their eyes strained to see the centerline on the road lit by the vehicle's headlights. They watched as sheets of sleet turned into waves of large snowflakes causing a near whiteout in front of the truck. Jack slowed to a crawl hugging each curve with precision and accuracy while Krista said a silent prayer, *"Father keep us safe and take away Sandy's anxiety. Thank You, God, for Jack's skillful driving. Amen,"* she said out loud. *"Amen,"* Jack answered.

After what seemed to take hours, they were out of the winding curves and more on the straightaway of the highway even though still hilly it was easier to drive. Their tension was loosening as they took deep cleansing breaths. The silence broke when Krista asked Jack where he learned his driving skills. To which he answered, he lived in the Ozarks all his life and had cut his teeth, so to speak, driving these treacherous roads in the hills long before he could legally drive a car.

"Did your parents know you were driving before you were licensed?" Krista asked, surprised that his parents would allow such a thing.

"Oh sure, my Dad taught me to drive when I was eight, I drove the tractor on the farm and his pickup hauling hay to the cows," Jack said, matter-of-factly.

She visualizes a little blond kid behind the steering wheel straining his neck to see ahead of him and stretching to reach the pedals.

"How did your dad die?"

"He was mowing the terrace out by the road and turned sharp and the ride-on mower turned over trapping him underneath. A neighbor found him and called the medics but he died shortly after they arrived. I would have mowed that terrace when I came home from school but a storm was brewing and my dad wanted it done before the rain came. Ironically, he basically drowned as the storm came in and filled the ravine where he was trapped face down."

"How awful Jack it must have been very hard for you knowing that you would have moved when you got home," Krista told Jack then her thoughts went to Sandy. "I pray that Brad is okay, I know Sandy is beside herself with worry. She said he collided helmet to helmet with another player. It sure doesn't sound good."

"No it doesn't but only God knows the outcome. We can pray for his mercy and healing power. We just have to put Brad in God's hands." Jack told Krista as they finally pulled into the parking lot of the hospital.

*****

Chatter filled the waiting room from down the hall at the nurse's station as the day shift gathered to review and discuss patient charts before going on duty. The doctors told Sandy earlier that the test results would take a couple of hours so they allowed her to talk to Brad briefly before taking him down the hall for a CT scan, the first of several tests to determine the extent of his injuries. Soon after their arrival, Krista prayed with her friend for patience and strength for the news to come, and then she turned Brad over to God.

The waiting was exhausting as the clock ticked away. Jack went to the hospital cafeteria to get some breakfast for the three girls. When he returned, Sandy introduced him to her ex-husband Harold, a strikingly handsome man who could easily be mistaken for a movie star and his wife Bobbitt several years his junior with a very young firm body encased in a very tight sweater. Jack handed the food to the girls then shook hands with Harold. They exchanged some small talk then stood as they saw the doctor come toward them. Krista took Sandy's hand and they braced for the doctor's report.

"I'm happy to report that the news is good. He has suffered a severely sprained neck and has a compressed vertebra that will need watching, but no spinal cord damage. He's a very fortunate young man. The muscle mass protected his neck as it sustained the impact. The helmet protected his head thus preventing a concussion. He will be very sore for a while until the inflammation subsides, but you can take him home. We put a neck brace on him to protect his neck until it heals and some muscle relaxers but other than that he's good to go."

Krista hugged Sandy and everyone cheered including the coach and players that kept a vigil in the waiting room with the family. The scene was harmonious as everyone realized that God heard their prayers and Brad would be all right. All the pent up emotions came pouring out as laughter began to replace tears and everyone hugged each other.

Jack turned to the group gathered in the waiting room and asked them to make a circle and hold hands. Sandy took Ginny's hand then Krista's leaving Harold to take Ginny's other hand. Then Jack offered gratitude to God. *"Father, we give you all the praise and glory for protecting Brad and bringing him through this experience with minor injuries. We ask you to bless Brad, his family, and friends and keep them safe on their journeys home. In Jesus' Name, we pray. Amen."* Giving him a hug, Sandy thanked Jack then he and Krista said their goodbyes and left the hospital.

"I called the pastor and told him we would not be there this morning. So we can take our time getting back and now it has stopped snowing so travel will be easier, the sun will be up before long and at least we will be able to see where we are sliding," he said with a chuckle. "What did Sandy think about you and me getting married?"

"I didn't tell her, Jack, I just couldn't share my good news while she was so worried. I'll tell her in a few days after things settle down a little in her life."

The trip back to Eureka Springs was tense over snow-covered roads but Jack managed to keep the truck on the road and in order to keep Krista from the tension he asked about her folks.

"My Mom died several years ago before Drew and I got married. It was hard to plan a wedding without her there to help me, you know, buy a dress, order the cake, and decorate for the reception and all of that. It was hard on my Dad too. She was sick for a long time and he was her caregiver. He took such good care of her. Dad was ten years older than she was and he retired early so he could be there in their home to take care of her. We lived in Tulsa and that is why I stayed and went to the University there, so I could help Dad and give him a little relief now and then."

"Were you close to your mom?"

"Yes, but because of her illness, we didn't do the things mothers and daughters do. She couldn't come to my graduation from High School or College, which was sad. When she died, it was as if a burden lifted from my shoulders. I'm sure you understand, even though Debbie was your wife, which is very different from a parent, still, after a long illness, there is a certain amount of relief. I had been grieving for a long time and did not recognize it until later. I missed so much growing up without both of my parents. For ten years, our lives revolved around caring for my mom. Then after we buried her, my dad just went downhill as if he gave up. Caregiving had been his whole existence and he didn't know anything else. So, two years after Drew and I said our vows my Dad had a stroke. He never recovered and died in a nursing home six months later.

I know this sounds awful Jack, but sitting in the waiting room of the hospital the night Drew died, I thanked God for taking him fast because I didn't want to go through what my dad did."

"That's not awful Krista, you saw what it did to him, but I'm sure you would have taken as good care of Drew as your dad did of your mom."

"I'm not sure about that…."

"What are you saying?"

"Maybe God didn't think I would be a good caregiver…"

"I don't believe that Krista, and here we are back safe and sound," he said pulling into his driveway after two hours on the road.

"You've never seen my cabin, have you?" Jack said.

"No, but it looks more like a house than a cabin."

"Well, I call it a cabin because that's what it started out to be. It isn't like your place, rustic and woodsy but it is made from logs, store-bought, not chopped but I would like to show it to you before I take you home."

"I would love to see it, and thank you for taking me home, I can not imagine driving on these roads myself."

Stomping her feet to release the snow from her boots, she entered the screened-in porch with Jack following close behind. He went ahead of her and unlocked the door. They entered a warm and cozy kitchen with a modern stove made to look like an antique. There was an abundance of cabinet space and the other appliances were up-to-date and fit the décor of the kitchen made to look like a farmhouse-style, eat-in kitchen. Jack took her coat hanging it on the coat rake next to the door and, after putting the teakettle on the stove, took her toward the dining room.

Much to her surprise, the dining room was furnished with antiques, complete with a large table, breakfront china cabinet, and the buffet was just what she would have picked for the room.

After they toured the rest of the house, Jack asked Krista to have lunch with him.

"I'll prepare some chili and you can throw together a salad. Okay?" Jack said, handing her some ingredients from the refrigerator.

"Chili sounds really good, do you have some crackers?"

"Yes up in the cabinet over the microwave."

After lunch, they worked side by side cleaning up the kitchen. At one point Jack put his arm around her waist and kissed her on the cheek, telling her how natural it felt to be together.

"Jack, do you believe in God's master plan?"

"Yes, I do and I further believe God put you in my life just at the right time. I needed you, Krista, to bring back my passion for life. The first time I laid eyes on you I knew something special was happening. Was it love at first sight? I don't know, but I know you brought me peace, and seeing you struggle with your grief helped me move on from my own grief. I believe that was God's intention, to get me off my pity party and use my experience to help someone else. It gave me a purpose and then one day I realized I was in love with you, something I didn't think would ever happen to me again. However, I'm ever so grateful that it has happened. We are very fortunate, you and I, to be able to love again Krista and I promise we will have a happy and full life together, forever."

"I love you, Jack, with all my heart."

Chapter 9

Christmas was everywhere and a very special time for Jack and Krista as they performed a cantata at their church on Christmas Day then went back to Krista's place to get presents and Goldie. They drove several miles to Berryville to have Christmas dinner with Jack's sister and family.

"I'm looking forward to meeting your sister and seeing the children. I hope to get a glimpse of what our children will look like. Do any of them resemble you?"

"I never thought much about it but now that you mention it, the youngest boy Joel looks a lot like I do in childhood pictures."

"Oh Jack, I want to see those pictures, are they at your sister's?"

"Yeah, some of them are, after Mom died we divided the pictures, so I have most of the ones of me."

It was not long until they were pulling into the driveway in front of his sister's house. Christmas lights outlined the small house and seasonal cutouts filled the lawn. Before they could get out of the truck kids surrounded them. Goldie ran around greeting everyone. Jack lifted Joel to his shoulder and swinging around grabbed both feet dangling around his neck. Joel giggled as Jack introduced him from his lofty height to Krista. Cara, the oldest, took Krista by the hand and led her to the front door where Jack's sister, Betty, clad in a bibbed apron protecting her new red pantsuit waited with open arms. Krista was awed by her beautiful smile and genuine friendliness. Betty immediately made her feel at home. It was like the first time she met Jack, comfortable and pleasant.

"Welcome, we are so glad you're here. Cara, take Krista's coat and put it on the bed in my room. Krista this is my husband Ben."

"Hello," Krista said. Ben was several inches shorter than Jack but muscular with the build of a football player.

"Hello yourself, well Jack she's a looker, can she cook?"

"She sure can, maybe not as good as me but she can learn," Jack said, teasing her as he put Joel on the floor then turning to wipe Goldie's paws before letting her inside.

"And this little shy one is Benjamin," Jack said leaning down in front of the young boy as he hid behind his mother.

"Hello Benjamin, I'm Krista and this is Goldie. She loves to be petted," she said as Benjamin reached a little hand out and stroked Goldie's head.

Delighted to be in a family with several children, Krista became acquainted with each one, learning their personalities and looking for recognition of Jack's traits in them. She and Betty were instant comrades sharing stories, recipes, likes, and dislikes while working together in the kitchen preparing the Christmas dinner, just like they had always known each other. The children played with their presents waiting for dinnertime. Krista noticed how well Jack related to the children and thought to herself what a wonderful father he would be. She mentioned her observation with Betty.

"Yes, I hope you have children because Jack is great with my kids and I know he wants his own. Oh, I'm sorry that was presumptuous of me to say that." Betty remarked with regret that she might have overstepped her bounds.

"Not at all, we are both anxious to have our own children, as a matter of fact, Jack said you had some pictures of him when he was a boy. I would love to see them."

Being sure the dinner was under control, Betty went to the bookcase and brought out several albums to show Krista. As the women went through the pictures, Jack and Ben soon joined them. Each flip of the page brought a better understanding of Jack's past. He and Betty talked about their growing up years including their brother, Mason, they had not heard from in many years. Krista asked about him as they viewed the years when Jack was in high school and the years after their father died.

"Mason was born when I was 10 years old and Betty was 8 so we were not that close to him. Betty baby-sat with him a lot, especially after Dad died and Mother went to work. He was a moody sort, not very open, and had a hard time expressing his feelings.

"Remember he had nightmares for months after Dad died," Jack said looking at Betty. "Then when Mother died, he left after the funeral and told us he was headed for Texas. We haven't heard from him since."

"He looks so unhappy in these pictures, like he's lost somehow, I don't know, sad maybe," Krista said staring at the picture of Mason's high school picture. "It must have been awful for him as young as he was and especially the way his Dad died, that is probably why he had nightmares, maybe he never got over it."

"Betty and I have talked about the fact that he never got counseling and how mother was in such grief it was hard for her to help him. So, she and Mason struggled, along with Betty and Jack, to accept what had happened and move on. Mason didn't know how to move on and his mother didn't want to, it was like she was afraid to let go of the memory for fear it would leave forever as he did." Ben said.

Krista listened intently to Betty's husband Ben's insight. "How sad for them both, I guess it didn't help much when you left for the armed service?" she said looking at Jack.

"Well, it put a strain on Betty, I look back now and know I could have done a lot of things differently, but I was just a kid, wet behind the ears and I wanted to get away from here as fast as I could, so the service was my ticket out. I'm not proud of the fact that I left my family to deal with everything. But I grew up. And when I came back, I helped as much as I could while going to college and keeping my grades up." Jack answered

"Don't be so hard on yourself Jack, you were hurting like we were and there was nobody to tell us what to do," Betty told him. "And you sent us money every month without fail and that helped a lot."

Krista watched the love between Betty and Jack and knew they were there for each other. She liked Jack's sister and looked forward to getting to know her better. Later she asked Betty to be in her wedding and she showed her some catalogs of vintage wedding dresses. She invited her to come to spend a couple of days in the Inn and see the vintage shop. Betty was excited to visit and she found herself very fond of her soon to be sister-in-law since neither woman had enjoyed the luxury of having a sister. Hopefully, this would bond them together.

With the meal ready for the table, they all gathered, and holding each other's hands, Ben asked the blessing on the food.

"Here, you and Jack can sit here," Ben said, pulling the chair out for Krista.

"Thank you, everything looks delicious, Betty," Krista complimented her new friend.

"Thank you, let's hope it tastes as good as it smells."

After dinner, much to Krista's surprise Jack and Ben cleaned up and washed the dishes. She and Betty retired to the living room where they could hear the football conversation coming from the kitchen.

"There is a football game, later on, that's why the boys are doing the dishes," Betty said quietly to Krista.

"You're kidding, does this happen often?"

"Only during football season, although in the summer they cook and I clean. So I guess we are even," she said with a chuckle.

Both women started laughing and the men peeked around the corner into the living room to see what was so funny.

"Are you laughing at us?" Jack asked.

"Of course, aren't you both the brunt of all laughter?" Betty said.

Later that evening they said their goodbyes and, with a promise to be back soon, loaded Goldie back in the truck, much against Benjamin's protest, and headed back to Eureka Springs. They shared their feelings from the day. Krista told of her observation of the sibling love Jack and Betty had for one another and she remarked that his brother-in-law, Ben, was a good husband and father. Jack was pleased that Krista saw the love and devotion in his family because that was what he wanted for their future. As he pulled up in front of Krista's front door, soft snowflakes began to fall. He helped Krista in with her gifts and empty dishes, then took Goldie out for a short walk looking around to make sure no one was lurking in the shadows, kissing her goodnight he said he would call the next day and they would go to the jewelers and order their rings. Krista did not want an engagement ring, just a wedding ring, so they designed a wide gold band with a large diamond set in the middle. Jack's ring would be a plain gold band. They decided to engrave the inside with 'the love of two hearts'.

Chapter **10**

Winter months produced ice and snow sometimes so severe that Eureka Springs shut down for days. Krista found herself stranded in the "ole Lady" for five straight days in January because a fast-moving system came across the Ozarks without warning and dumped 12 inches of snow on top of a half-inch of ice making the roads impassable and Jack could not come into town. During that time, she worked in the store dusting, arranging, and ordering for the spring. She and Jack decided to have a May wedding with a vintage theme. She looked through catalogs for just the right dress for herself and her matron of honor, Sandy and bridesmaid, Betty and junior bridesmaids, Ginny and Cara. Krista hoped that the Schmidts would return in time for the wedding.

She and Jack talked endlessly on their cell phones about wedding plans and their future together. He told her what to check on in the Inn because of the low temperature, and cautioned her about walking outside with Goldie.

"Just let her go out by herself, she is used to keeping her balance and will come back where it is warm."

"Yes, Sir ...I'll let her out by herself ...I love you. Thank you for watching out for me."

"And don't even try to shovel snow off the sidewalk in front of the shop. No one will be shopping and you may slip and break something."

"I promise to be a good girl…okay?" she told him thinking how she would never be able to shovel all the snow in front of the shop even if she wanted to, because if she opened the door the piled up snow would blow into the shop making a huge mess. The winds would howl night and day between the buildings making deeper snowdrifts. She would let Goldie out the door of her living quarters because the winds had blown the snow away from the porch piling it against her car parked at the end of the porch. Goldie would run out, find a spot, and shake the snow from her fur run back in as Krista watched from the door.

"Good girl, here let me wipe your paws, that a girl, now you're all dry," she would say each time her companion came in from the snow.

The Red Lady Inn

One afternoon she decided to spruce up the display window, rearrange products and redress the manikins. She found the dresses and accessories to use, then climbed onto the stage of the display window; she carefully laid the items across the antique cane chair. Taking the clothing off the manikins was proving to be more difficult in the small space. She began to reposition herself and while turning she looked up to find herself face to face with a man staring at her through the glass. Startled, she lost her balance and fell backward off the window stage. Grabbing for the curtains that hung on the back of the stage, she managed to slow her fall. Then as her head crashed against the edge of the counter, she felt her brain detach as it moved inside her head. Finally, she came to a stop with a cracking sound on the concrete floor. Her eyes closed, she lay still trying to catch her breath, she realized she was hurt, her leg ended up under her and she knew her ankle was broken. Her head was pounding in rhythm to her heartbeat. Goldie began to bark and lick Krista in the face.

She looked up to see if the man was still at the window. Not seeing him anywhere she realized her predicament and fear set in. Unable to get help, tears began to roll down her cheeks. Nauseated from the severe pain, she tried to drag herself toward the counter where the phone lay just out of her reach. Pulling her badly broken ankle closer to her, and with one hand stretched out in front of her as far as she could, she reached for the cell phone on top of the counter. But, the throbbing pain was unbearable and she put her head down on the outstretched arm in defeat. The thought passed through her mind that she could be there for days. She began to tremble and realized she was going into shock.

Her brain tried to untangle thoughts that crowded together intertwined with warnings from Jack and delays in opening the Inn. Goldie lay down beside her as the trembling got worse licking her hand on the outstretched arm. When Krista moaned, Goldie barked as if to say she was helping. Then Goldie started loud continuous barking then running in circles.

"What is it, Girl?" Krista mumbled inaudibly, coming back to reality from the confusion of what seemed like a deep sleep, to excruciating pain that made her faint again.

Goldie's constant barking broke the cycle of in and out of consciousness. In a distance, she could hear sirens, coming closer she held her breath and prayed they somehow knew she was in trouble. Then suddenly the emergency unit stopped in front of the Inn. The red flashing lights threw big red circles of shadows on the walls. She saw through the window two familiar faces, one of them being Bud. They ran up to the door and tried to open it, finding it locked, Bud called out to Krista. She tried to answer that she was hurt, but they couldn't hear her over Goldie barking and lunging at the door. One paramedic shoveled through the snowdrift while Bud, assuring that Krista was away from the door, broke the pane window. Turning the key, Krista had left in the deadbolt; they managed to come in nearly falling on the slippery floors now covered with snow. They found her lying on the floor in a pool of blood.

"What happened?" Bud asked, tending to her badly broken ankle.

"Someone was looking in the window… and it startled me… I fell back … hit my head and landed on top of my ankle." She said weakly gasping for breath. For the first time, Krista saw the blood from the wound on her head and feeling as if she could not breathe, she went blank and passed out.

Bud wrapped her head with a pressure bandage, stabilized the compound fracture in her ankle, and prepared to transport her to the hospital. With a neck brace in place, they put her on the gurney and managed to take her through the snow and in the emergency unit where she came back awake, long enough to ask how they knew she was hurt.

"We got a call from a man saying he saw you fall out of the display window and thought you might be hurt. Now just relax, you're going to be fine." Bud said in his best bedside manner as he attached monitors to her chest and legs, and started an IV line. The Unit began to move and Bud talked to the hospital, telling them what was going on with his patient, not forgetting, his best friend's fiancée.

Krista, going in and out of consciousness, asked Bud to tell Jack, but "do not scare him," she said just as they pulled into the driveway at the hospital. "I'll take care of it, Krista, I promise, you just concentrate on staying calm. Okay?" She nodded.

As soon as he could, Bud called Jack and told him that Krista was in surgery to repair a compound fracture of her ankle. Jack asked a few questions and said he would be there as soon as possible. Bud told him to wait and let him come get him because they had chains on the Emergency Unit but Jack said he would make it and not to take the Unit out that far from town.

Jack was not about to wait patiently for Bud to come out and take him back to the hospital. He put on his boots, heavy coat, gloves grabbed two blankets, and a hand full of chocolate bars in case he slid off the road then waded in the deep snow to his truck. Spinning the tires a few times, he managed to get out of the driveway.

It was not an easy trip as the snow was so deep he had a hard time seeing the road. Determined to get to the hospital, he kept his wits about him and slowly maneuvered the curves flanked on one side by steep ravines with trees the only thing stopping him if he went off the road. The windshield wipers worked hard to move the ice made worse by low one-digit temperatures as it built up with every squirt of the wiper fluid. Jack strained to see and found his muscles so tight that he could hardly move. He began to talk aloud to God praying for Krista then safety for himself while slowing down for each curve. At one point, he missed the road entirely. Determination and faith pulled his truck temporarily trapped in a snowbank, back on the road. With God by his side, he began to relax.

When he finally arrived at the hospital, it had been two hours since Bud had called. Krista was out of surgery with three pins in her ankle and stitches in her head. She still had a collar on her neck for the whiplash she had sustained when her head hit the counter. Heavily sedated, she was unaware that Jack was there keeping vigil. He felt so helpless watching her lay there in so much pain. She would wake long enough to ask for something for the pain, then she would go back to sleep.

The next day, Jack felt like he could leave Krista while he went to check on Goldie and fix the door. When he arrived, he found someone had boarded the window in the door of the shop and Goldie whining ready for Jack to open the door.

"She's okay girl, come on let's go outside and then I'll get you something to eat."

He let Goldie outside in the snow and watched her as she went in the street and followed the tracks a few steps from the Inn. She looked back at Jack then pushing her way into the snow, she completed her duty and ran back to where he had a towel ready to wipe her paws. Hugging her neck he said, "thank you, ole girl, for taking care of our friend, she is going to be okay and back with us soon."

Back at the hospital, he saw Bud who was there with another patient and asked if he had boarded the door. "No, we went back to fix it and locked it up, and let Goldie out, but it was already done. It was strange we never saw anyone around. I wonder who called us."

"Yes, I wonder about that myself. She told you it was a man standing outside the window. What was he doing outside the window, in the snowdrifts looking in?" Jack asked.

Bud shook his head. "It is a mystery alright, the whole thing is strange."

In Krista's room, he held her hand and told her how sorry he was that he wasn't there to help her. She did not say much as the pain killers were strong and kept her pretty much out of it for a couple of days. Jack stayed by her side leaving only to check on Goldie. He watched her grimace with pain and wiped away her tears when she got concerned about the Inn and their wedding. He assured her that everything would work out all right and they should count their blessings.

"It could have been a lot worse Krista, I can't even think about what would have happened if the stranger had not called the firehouse and I believe Bud would have walked to help you if they had not been able to get through with the Unit. Thank God you're alright, I love you, Krista Moore."

"I love you too Jack Nolan," Krista said, forcing a smile. "Remember God is in charge, always. Even when we don't understand why, we know He's in charge."

"Amen, you're so right Krista, there must be a reason for this delay in our plans. We just have to trust God with it. I want to hold you but I can wait until you're better which will be real soon."

*****

In a few days, they released Krista from the hospital and Jack took her home where Goldie was very glad to see her. Barking and wagging her tail she let Krista know how much she missed her.

"Tell me again about this guy in the window the day you got hurt," Jack said, helping her take off her coat.

"Well, I was working in the window and I got a chill, you know like something was wrong and when I looked up there he was staring at me through the glass."

"You didn't recognize him?"

"No."

"What did he look like?"

"Well, he was tall because we were nearly eye to eye and I was standing on the stage of the window. He was wearing a dark parka with the hood covering his head and I noticed his hands in his pockets. I wonder why he was out in that weather. His face was unshaven but he didn't have a long beard and he seemed to be rather thin."

Molly Owen

"Would you recognize him if you saw him again?"

"I don't think so. It just happened too fast."

"At least the guy had sense enough to call 911 or else you could have laid there a while. I would have called 911 myself if you hadn't answered the phone."

"I was so grateful when I heard the sirens, Jack, I must admit I was pretty scared and in a lot of pain. He must have had a cell phone otherwise he wouldn't have been able to call anyone."

Jack kissed her forehead and went to the kitchen to put on some coffee. He came back with a proposal. In anticipation of her condition, he brought enough clothes to stay a while and suggested that he sleep on the couch until she was able to get around better by herself. She was glad he offered because she was not anxious to be alone just yet.

Without letting on to Krista, Jack had another reason for staying close by, he was concerned about the appearance of the man in front of her shop on a miserable cold winter day in knee-high drifts of snow. Each incident in itself was not disturbing but now there were three different sightings of a strange man around the Inn. He was not sure that all three were the same man but it was beginning to look like someone was stalking Krista for reasons unknown to him. He had alerted the local police to be on the lookout for anything strange happening around or near the Inn.

*****

The sun finally came out and soon the snow had melted off the roads leaving the remains of melting snow drifts everywhere. Jack shoveled snow off the sidewalk in front of the shop, repaired the window in the door then managed to remove the snow from the porch upstairs and the roof. In a few days, there was little sign of a snowstorm. Jack replenished the food supply and left Krista long enough to drive to his place and make sure everything was okay.

On his return, he found Bud sitting on the porch. "Hey, man what are you doing out here in the cold?"

"I didn't want to disturb Krista and I knew you wouldn't leave her for long, so I just waited. How's she doing?"

"Well, come in and see for yourself," he said opening the door. "Look who I found lurking on the porch."

"Hi Bud, I must have fallen asleep, did you knock?"

"No, I just waited for Jack."

"Well, have a seat while our gracious host gets us something to drink, I would but as you can see I'm a little preoccupied. By the way, thank you again for getting here so fast and taking such good care of me. I can't tell you how much I appreciate what you did. I kept thinking I knew you from somewhere then when we were at the cabin I remembered you were the paramedic that came out for my husband Drew and I want to thank you for that too."

"You're very welcome," Bud said, taking the beer Jack handed him. "It scared me when we got that call because I knew it was you and I didn't know what we would find when we got here. I'm just glad you're on the mend. Goldie was a big help, she let us know you were hurt and encouraged us to hurry."

"She tried to keep me warm lying down beside me. I was shaking and I'm sure it scared her," she said watching Bud stroke Goldie's fur.

"Say Bud, how about staying for dinner, I'm grilling up some steaks and I hear you're a pretty good cook so you can mix up some salad greens and put some potatoes in the oven, how's that sound?"

"Pretty good, lead the way master, I'm all yours."

Krista was enjoying watching them from the couch as Jack doctored the steaks and Bud started the salad after setting the oven for the potatoes. They went outside, Goldie following close behind, not forgetting to check back with her master to get an okay as they started the grill. She heard them laughing and was glad Bud had come by to take Jack's mind off her disability for a little while. She knew how concerned Jack was and she must admit she was concerned too. Would she be able to walk soon? The doctor kept reassuring them but she still had a lot of pain and he told her it would be several weeks for her to be back to normal. She then noticed the conversation outside had turned more serious.

"Carrie called me yesterday, right out of the blue," Bud said.

"What did she want?" Jack said, turning the steaks on the grill.

"I'm not sure, she said she had been thinking about me and ran into an old friend that told her I was here in Eureka Springs working for the fire department and just wanted to see how I was doing. But, I got the feeling that there was more to it than that."

"In what way?"

"You know, asking questions like — are you married? do you have any kids?—stuff like that," Bud said, hoping Jack could shed some light on his conversation.

"Sounds like what anyone would ask, after all, it has been, what, ten, twelve years, since before you enlisted. A lot happens in that amount of time. Did you ask her anything about her life over the past several years?"

"Yes, but she avoided any direct answer, kinda hedged a little like she didn't want to tell me. Maybe it was just my imagination, but Jack I've got to tell you, just the sound of her voice made my heart go pitter-pat as they say, and I can't get her off my mind. After all this time, I think I still love her and maybe that's why I haven't been able to find the right one."

"What if she's married? Did she say anything about kids?"

"No, not..., like I said she was very vague."

Molly Owen

"Sounds like she's hiding something, is she back living in Berryville?"

"She didn't say."

"Betty would say you're a typical male, not asking questions."

"And she would probably be right, but I sure wish I had more answers," he said helping Jack take in the steaks.

Jack set up the TV tray for Krista then he and Bud served the plates. "You two can sit at the counter, you'll be more comfortable," Krista said.

"We will be just fine at the TV trays; anyway we want to eat in the same room as you," Jack said as they sat down and bowed their heads.

"Dear Father, we thank you so much for people like Bud out there every day helping people and we are so grateful he was there for Krista. Thank you for the doctors' skills that took such good care of Krista. We ask for your healing power, Father. We love you and we pray this in the Name of your precious son, Jesus Christ. Amen."

"Amen," Krista and Bud said in unison.

With small talk in-between bites, they were soon ready for dessert. Jack brought out the ice cream and scooped it into bowls, then drizzled it with chocolate sauce.

"Boy, I'll come here more often for dinner if I get ice cream for dessert."

"You're welcome anytime," Krista said, taking a final bite.

Bud helped Jack clean up and then said his goodbyes leaving Jack and Krista alone to contemplate their future while waiting for Krista to heal.

"Bud is a good friend, isn't he?"

"Yes, he's one of the best. He would lay down his life for me, as a matter of fact, he did at one point save my life."

"When was that? What happened? Was it an accident?"

"Hold everything missy, when you start shooting questions at me so fast, I can't even remember what you asked, let alone which one came first, " he said grinning.

"Well, hurry up and tell me, I'm dying here, waiting."

He began with a little background information, telling her how he and Bud were close in high school and had each other's back no matter what. They did things together all the time from sports to automobiles to double dates. He and Debbie were sweethearts and Bud was dating a girl by the name of Carrie. It was their practice to take turns driving on double dates. Jack's car was an old Ford Coupe that he had practically rebuilt and lately he was having trouble keeping the air in the tires. It was his turn to take his car so he aired the tires and away they went. Most of the action was out on 62 so they headed out on the highway without a care in the world when suddenly one of the old tires blew and Jack barely kept them from going off the road, "which around here would have certainly been fatal." He told her then continued.

"I got out of the car and assessed the damage. I had a spare, so telling the girls to get out of the car and rest by the tree, I took the tire jack and laying on my back began to scoot under the car to place the jack on the axle. I moved back out and started pumping the jack. Then, the car started to lean on the uneven slope. I got back under the car to adjust the jack when suddenly the car shifted and fell on top of me pinning me underneath. I heard the girls scream and then felt pain in my leg. Bud, calm as a cucumber, told me to hold on and he took the tire iron and began to pump then told me to scoot out from under the car. After several tries and with brute force he held the car up far enough for me to maneuver enough to get out from underneath. When he let the car down it went all the way down and would have surely crushed me."

"Oh Jack, that would have been awful, so Bud is a hero."

"He says that is why he decided to become a paramedic. He served in the army as a medic on the front line."

"Wow, that is fascinating. Did you serve in the army with him?"

"No, we were stationed at different posts and served overseas with different units. We never saw each other during our service but got back together after we returned stateside. We both considered staying in you know making a career out of the military. However, Debbie was waiting for me to get out so we could get married. Carrie…well, she didn't wait for Bud, married someone else and moved away from here…so Bud decided to apply at the firehouse in Berryville and then ended up in Rogers for several years. He was glad when an opening came up here in Eureka Springs. He loves what he does and he's good at it."

"We are lucky to have him here in Eureka Springs, I feel better knowing he's here, don't you?"

"I do, it is getting late Hon and we better start getting you ready for bed."

"You're so right, I'm tired tonight and I don't know why. I haven't done anything in days but it seems more like months. As much as I appreciate your help Jack and I do, I'll be so glad when I can do it for myself again," she said as Jack helped her up from the couch. Once standing he put his arms around her then leaned down and kissed her passionately.

"It won't be long, you'll see. Just do what the doctor says and you will be back to normal soon, I promise," Jack said, helping her to the bedroom.

Chapter *11*

In the middle of the week, Sandy arrived unannounced. Knocking at the door, she heard Krista call out.

"Who's there?"

"It's me Krista, Sandy."

"Oh, Sandy, come on in," Krista said, propping herself up on pillows.

"I didn't wake you did I?"

"Oh no, I have become part of this couch, like one of its cushions. What on earth are you doing over here midweek?"

"I had some time and decided to see for myself how you're doing, plus I ran across a wedding planner in Rogers and she gave me some great ideas. I thought you and I could talk about the wedding and get your mind off your situation with the couch, which I'm sure you detest at this point. Are you game?"

"What a wonderful idea and it will give Jack a break, bless him, he has been so good Sandy, I don't know what I would have done without him and he still wants to marry me after seeing me at my very worst," Krista confided.

"Of course he does and yes you're very fortunate to have him here. By the way, where is he anyway?"

"Well, once he gets me settled he goes to the store, then to check on his place. Honestly, it takes him maybe an hour and he's a bundle of nerves until he returns. I have an emergency thing around my neck to directly call the fire station and I'm not about to try anything foolish, like get off this confounded couch. So I don't understand his concern."

"He loves you, silly."

Soon Jack was back and very glad to see Sandy. He put the groceries away and asked if she would stay for lunch. When she told him she planned to spend the day and he could take some personal time while she stayed and helped Krista, he jumped at the chance even though he gave a little resistance. He gave Sandy some instructions and his cell number in case there were any problems. Then kissing Krista on the forehead he grabbed his supply list and headed out the door.

It was hard to concentrate on purchases at the hardware store, always being in a rush to get back to Krista, so usually, he would just grab something and end up having to return it. As he entered the store, he headed straight for the electrical department, looking at his list as he went along. Suddenly, with his head down, he bumped into someone. "Sorry," he said, glancing at the tall figure then moving on.

Walking down the aisle, he found what he was looking for and picked up some other items he thought he might need later. As he headed for the plumbing department, he could not shake a familiar feeling. *Who was that, do I know him?* He thought. Looking around he could not find him and finally pushed it out of his mind.

One final stop to get paint and he was headed for the cashier. Several isles over, again, he saw the figure he had bumped into before. The man had his back to him and a shirt with the hood over his head. *Wait a minute, is he the guy that keeps showing up around the Inn?* Jack impatiently tried to hurry the cashier, all the time keeping an eye on the hooded man. Finally, he grabbed his bag and hurried out the door looking out in the parking lot, looking left, then right. The man was nowhere around leaving Jack frustrated. He went to his car still looking around, backed out of the parking place, and headed for the street. Just as he turned right onto the street, he caught a glimpse of the man walking the other way about a block away. He kept him in his rearview mirror until he could turn around. However, just as in the parking lot he lost him again.

Molly Owen

Even though it was a vague sighting, he decided to tell Bud. Arriving at the fire station, he saw Bud in the kitchen and went in.

"Hey Jack, what are you doing here? Is Krista okay?"

"Yes, Sandy is with her. I just wanted you to know that I think I saw that guy again, you know the one who I think has been stalking Krista. Somehow he looks familiar, but I can't quite figure out who he is or where I've seen him before, except for the times he has been around the Inn. He was in the Hardware Store and I tried to follow him but he got away from me. I spotted him again, but he was walking the opposite way and I couldn't turn around fast enough. I drove up and down in the block, but you know how it is around here he could get on a trail on one street and end up way over on another street entirely."

"Tell me about it, our emergency unit can't get there from here half the time."

"I'm sure that is how he gets around so fast, he walks or runs from one place to another using the trails up and down the hillsides."

"I'll tell the fellows and it might be a good idea to tell the police where you saw him so we can keep an eye out for him," Bud told Jack.

"Thanks, Bud, I better get back to the Inn."

"Hi ladies, how are we doing?" Jack said, putting his packages on the counter. "I see we had lunch."

"Oh Jack, I'm sorry, do you want me to fix you something?" Sandy said getting up.

"You sit right down there, I can get myself something to eat. Looks like you have a plan in mind for the wedding."

"Jack, it's going to be beautiful, Sandy has some great ideas. Do you want to see them?"

"Not right now, while Sandy is here I'm going to finish some projects downstairs, maybe you can show me tonight," Jack said, stuffing the rest of the sandwich in his mouth and heading for the stairs. "And Krista?"

"Yes."

"I love you and you will be all I'm looking at when we get married."

Later that afternoon Sandy needed to get home before dark and after calling downstairs to tell Jack she was leaving, she gave Krista a hug, gathered the leftover ideas up, and put them in her tote bag.

"I'll call you soon," Sandy told Krista.

"Thank you, Sandy, this was great fun….have a safe trip."

Just then, there was a knock at the door. "Hello, Bud," Sandy said as she opened the door.

Molly Owen

"Hello yourself, where are you going in such a hurry? I thought I would take the innkeepers out to dinner, you want to come along?"

Anxious to get home she thanked Bud for the invite and told him maybe next time when she didn't need to get back to teenagers and animals.

"Well, I'll excuse you this time, but the four of us should do dinner sometime."

"Yes, sounds good, goodbye Krista, talk to you later," Sandy said, pushing passed Bud in the doorway as he held the screen door open. She made a mental note that Bud seemed nicer, not so full of himself like the last time they met.

"Where's Jack?" Bud said, looking around.

"He's coming, he was downstairs locking up. So where are we going for dinner?" Krista asked, anxious to go out anywhere.

"Your choice."

"How about that catfish place up on highway 62. I can't remember the name? I know you and Jack love the place and I've been hungry for catfish myself." Krista said getting up from the couch with a little help from Bud, as he handed her the crutches.

"Hey man, where are you going with my girl?" Jack said coming through the door and into the living room.

"Down big fellow, I thought you two needed a night out and I'm here to take you," Bud said, still holding on to Krista as she adjusted her crutches under her arms.

"Isn't that sweet, Jack?" Krista grinned.

"Hmmm, sure and what do you want for this act of kindness?"

"Jack!" Krista scolded.

"Don't worry your pretty little head, Krista, Jack is just upset that he didn't come up with the idea first."

"I'll be just a minute. I've got to wash up," Jack said.

"Take your time I'll keep Krista entertained," Bud teased.

Soon they were out the door, promising Goldie they would return soon watching her as she stared out the window. Jack helped Krista into the cab of Bud's pickup then got in the back seat. They took off through town until they reached the highway and headed west. Pulling into the driveway in front of the Restaurant, Bud let Krista and Jack out at the door then went to park. Soon they found a table in the corner and placed their order.

The dessert menu showed a picture of a piece of apple pie a la mode and all three couldn't resist. The waitress set the dishes down in front of them and as they were voicing their satisfaction, a female voice called out.

"I don't believe it. Jack and Bud right before my eyes."

"Well, hello Carrie, long time no see, how've you been? This is my fiancée Krista." Jack said as he and Bud stood up.

"Hello," Krista said smiling.

Bud was still standing when Jack sat down. He could not take his eyes off Carrie. She was more beautiful than in high school. Her long blonde hair cascaded over her bare shoulders and his eyes followed the rest of her slim curvy body down her long legs until Jack kicked him under the table.

"You care to join us?" Bud said looking around for some hunk she may be with that was watching his schoolboy tactics of flirting.

"No thanks, I'm here with some friends, just wanted to say hello, it is nice meeting you Krista. Betty has told me all about you." Carrie said turning and smiling at Jack then looking up at Bud who was still standing and said. "See you around, Bud."

When Bud finally sat down, he looked like he had seen a ghost. He took a big sip of coffee drooling it off his chin as he turned and looked again in Carrie's direction.

"Wow, I think I'm in love. Did you see that? She is gorgeous, I mean she was always a looker but wow, she is all grown up." Bud said to the air.

Krista could not help herself, she began to laugh and covering her mouth with her hand, she stifled another snort as she tried to quit laughing. Tears began to run down her face as Jack joined her in hysterical laughter. Bud was so engrossed in staring at the backside of Carrie as she walked, hips swaying, across the room and out the door that he did not notice their complete lack of control. As Bud came back to reality, they were still trying to stop their behavior.

"What? What's so funny?" Bud said.

"You are man, if I didn't know better, I would say you just got out of middle school. Get a hold of yourself, pull in your tongue, and close your mouth. You look like an old hound dog chasing a poodle." Jack said still lacking any control himself from the side-splitting hysteria still lurking around the table.

"I don't believe it, she was flirting with me. She was flirting with me, wasn't she? I didn't just dream this, did I? She was right here, in front of me, by the way, so close I could smell her perfume," he said with a smirk on his face as he took in a deep breath and closed his eyes as if he could still smell the lingering aroma.

"Jack, I think he may pass out any minute. Breathe, Bud, breathe," Krista said, starting to laugh again. "I haven't laughed this hard in months, no years. It's wonderful. Thank you, Bud, I needed that. Even though it took you making a fool out of yourself, it was worth it."

"It's wonderful, isn't it?" Bud said, swirling his fork around in his apple pie mixing it with melted ice cream with no intention of eating it.

Molly Owen

"He's a goner, Krista, we've lost him," Jack said. "He's drunk on love."

When Bud drove them back to the Inn, he helped Jack with Krista, then hurried back to his pick-up and, waving, sped down the road as if called to a fire. Jack shook his head as he and Krista settled into the rocking chairs on the front porch. There was a cool breeze and Krista pulled her jacket tight around her shoulders. Jack let Goldie out and walking her in the opposite direction from the garden took her down the road. Krista watched as they turned the corner but not out of sight, so Jack could still see her. After Goldie had a tour of the familiar and not so familiar smells, they returned to the porch where Goldie lay down at Krista's feet.

Looking around her, the forsythias would soon be in full bloom with brilliant yellow foliage followed by the blossoms of the redbud trees and the dogwoods sprinkling their foliage throughout the woods surrounding the Inn.

"We need to make a trip to the garden center soon. I would like to hang some baskets in between the posts on the porch and we need more perennials in the garden and the urns in front of the shop need new plantings now that spring is coming," Krista said.

"Remember, we can still get a cold snap, don't want to put things out too early. When we do start planting, I'll have my work cut out for me. But I think you're right, and remember it won't be long until you can get in the garden and get your hands dirty," Jack reminded her.

"I can't wait, I'm so ready to shed these crutches and get on with my life…our life," she said with a quick smile.

As the sun began to set and the fireflies flashed in the coming darkness, bats began their evening flights from the cave high on the hill across the road looking for their dinner of fresh insects. They sat in silence for a very long time absorbing the atmosphere to its fullest, watching nature unfold before them. In the distance, they heard the bells ring out from the steeple at the church behind the Crescent Hotel sounding the time with each gong.

"Do you think Bud and Carrie will get back together?" Krista asked softly as not to startle their surroundings.

"I don't know, could be, I don't think Bud knows much about where Carrie has been these past several years. She was married when he came back from the service, so — is she still married? , divorced?, or what is going on with her? — he's going to have a very hard time with this no matter what the answer is to those questions."

"How so?" Krista asked.

"I guess because he never stopped loving her and she didn't wait for him and now she seems to be pursuing him. That can only make it hard to know what to do and how to do it. When she called him, he didn't ask too many questions and I bet right now he wishes he had."

*****

Bud drove around town searching in hopes of catching a glimpse of her again, maybe finding out where she was staying. He had not felt this way since he was in high school. As many women as he had known through the years, not one made him feel the way Carrie did. The spark was still there and he desperately wanted to pursue a relationship with her again. In total denial, he chose not to think about her past or present for that matter. He just wanted to start all over as if the years between had not even happened. If he could not find her, he would call Betty and see if she knew where Carrie was staying. He assumed the friends she spoke of earlier were girlfriends. Driving downtown where all the teens drove their cars up and down the main drag, he moved over to let a jeep pass on the other side when he heard his name.

"Bud, up here," Carrie shouted.

Looking around he saw her practically hanging over the banister of the balcony in front of the New Orleans Hotel.

"Hey, he shouted back at her."

"Bud, come on up, I'll meet you downstairs in front."

He drove up the street pulled into a side street and turned around. As luck would have it, a parking place was across the street from the hotel and he backed in parallel parking like a pro not scraping one tire. Jumping out he did not notice the car coming around the curve and with the horn blaring and the kid behind the wheel shouting a few choice words, he pulled back in time to avoid a direct hit. Carrie stood on the sidewalk laughing. All his efforts to impress with his parking skill went out the window as all attention was on him, from every direction people stared at the fellow that did not pay attention and barely avoided death by a hit and run driver.

Carrie took his hand and led him up the staircase to the rooms on the second floor, where she introduced him to two of her girlfriends and reaching inside the cooler, she handed him a beer. The four of them sat on the balcony watching the cars passing by until Bud said he had to get some sleep before his shift started at the firehouse.

Carrie walked him to the door of the room and leaned in for a kiss.

"Not a good idea Carrie," Bud said, pulling back.

"Why not Bud, you know you want to," Carrie said, pouting.

"We will need to fill in a few gaps from the past decade before we can go there and you're right I want to kiss you but not yet," he said, surprising himself.

"What do you want from me, Bud, an apology for not waiting four long years for you? Why didn't you ask me to marry you before you left? You and Jack just left Debbie and me waiting, well I didn't wait but now I'm here and you know we are right for each other."

"Not yet, Carrie, we need to talk, we can't just pick up from where we left off, there is more to it than that. When I saw you tonight at the café I thought I could forget and I didn't need to know what, where, and why but now I realize I do need to know, so when you're ready to sit down with me and talk you know where to find me," Bud said walking out the door never looking back.

As he went across the street to his truck, he wondered what had gotten into him. He did not know he had it in him to put a relationship with the only girl he had ever cared about on hold until he knew more. *What difference did it make? What is done is done,* he thought, then turning the key, the motor roared as he cranked the steering wheel, pulled away from the curb and headed for the highway.

Chapter **12**

Several weeks passed as Krista recuperated. Now in a walking boot to protect her ankle, she was able to do more around the Inn as she prepared for the grand opening. Jack had worked hard while taking care of Krista to get the garden ready and finish the painting inside. Their wedding planning on hold until after the opening, Krista still dreamed over pages of wedding catalogs for the perfect dress for herself and dresses for her attendants. Determined to walk down the aisle in regular shoes she convinced Jack to postpone the wedding until July.

The excitement was building as they looked forward to the grand opening of The Red Lady Inn. The Schmidts, back from Texas, were helping the couple with the finishing touches. Krista planned to prepare the baked goods herself to serve to the occupants of the bed and breakfast but unable to be on her feet that long, Mrs. Schmidt offered to do the baking until she was able to do it herself. The rooms were already reserved for the next few weeks after much advertising.

Bud was helping Jack with last-minute fix-its and Sandy brought Ginny with her to help put toiletries in all the bathrooms and make sure enough towels, washcloths and terry cloth robes were in place. Mirrors cleaned, pillows puffed, rugs swept and rose-scented oil applied to all the light bulbs in the antique lamps brought the whole ambiance together.

Krista found herself frustrated with her lack of mobility and her emotions took over in fits of tears. Everyone was understanding and patient with her knowing how difficult it was for her to see her dream come true only to be unable to participate at the last minute detailing. Jack reassured her that everything would be great and she would soon be back to normal and running up and down the stairs again.

Jack gathered the helpers together for prayer, taking Krista's hand, everyone else held hands in a circle around Krista, *"Our heavenly Father, thank you for our many friends who have come to help us today. We praise you, Father, for giving us strength at this time as we prepare to open the Inn. Thank you for Your healing power over Krista and Jesus, give her peace and courage as we present her dream to the public. We are so blessed that we have reservations already and that You have and will continue to walk with us as we welcome guests. Our faith is in You, Lord.*

Please keep everyone safe as they travel to and from. We love you, Lord. In Jesus' name, Amen.

Krista thanked Jack for the prayer, then she thanked everyone in the room around her. Anxious to get them back to work, she asked Jack, "Did you remember fresh roses and chocolates in the rooms?"

"Actually, I have the vases and flowers ready for you to arrange. Then I'll put them in the rooms with the heart-shaped chocolate boxes," Jack told her, later surprising her with pictures of each room.

"Those are perfect…we could use these for advertising, thank you, Jack."

Valentine's Day was the opening day for The Red Lady Inn and all advertising and décor was centered on the romance of Cupid's Day from the first level at Victoria's to the top level on the porch in front of Krista's living quarters and the gardens outside. Heart-shaped soaps adorned the pedestal sinks in the bathrooms. Framed cupids and angels hung on the walls. Yards of draped lace hung from crowns over the beds. Wicker bed trays rested on top of vintage bed coverings inviting breakfast in bed, and the scent of roses permeated the rooms. Vintage linen tablecloths covered the bedside tables topped with oil lamps converted to electric lamps. The beautiful antique buffet sat in the large hall on the second floor ready for the silver trays full of Mrs. Schmidt's baked goods in the morning.

Molly Owen

Flowers and chocolates in place, Jack went downstairs to welcome the guest at the registration desk in the back of Victoria's. He brought Krista to the lower level in her car. She sat proudly behind the desk taking information, and giving out ribbon tied keys to their matching room color from the pegboard that hung on the wall behind her. No detail was too small and every detail was accomplished with great care.

Watching each couple climb the old staircase to their romantic getaway, she thanked God for the opportunity to put happiness into their lives. She wondered if, in some way, renewed commitments were being made or perhaps they were newlyweds beginning their life together as she and Drew had many years ago. Suddenly she envied them and remembered, in the busyness of the opening, she had almost forgotten that soon she and Jack would begin their life together in this very same Inn.

"Krista, did you hear me?" Bud said, carrying a large box.

"Oh, I'm sorry, I was lost in thought."

"Where do you want this? Jack has a few more coming."

"Let's put them over there until I can open them and mark the items. Thank you so much for your help, Bud. We appreciate it."

"You're quite welcome, anything for friends."

"Speaking of friends…..what were you telling me outside about Carrie? I couldn't hear you for the truck motor," Jack said coming through the door and setting more boxes down.

"Oh nothing, I haven't heard from her since the night I was with her at the New Orleans Hotel down on Main Street," Bud said.

"You slept with her at the New Orleans hotel?" Krista said horrified.

"No. No, I didn't. Jack didn't tell you? I didn't sleep with her, I didn't even let her kiss me….can you believe it. I gave her an ultimatum that we needed to talk before we could have a relationship. I don't think she was too happy about it. But I just couldn't go any further without knowing what was going on with her, you know, marriage, kids, all those things that a person needs to know about another person before he makes a fool of himself….again."

"I see, so why hasn't she called you?" Krista said.

"You tell me. Maybe her secrets are too hard to admit to or maybe she was just looking for a one night stand and thought I was an easy mark, I don't know and I'm beginning not to care."

"Watching you that night at the café, I can't believe you don't want to see her again," Jack said winking at Krista.

"I do. But don't you think I'm right about this?"

"We do, Bud, and I for one am proud of you. If you're meant to be with her, then it will happen, we'll pray about it," Krista said.

Molly Owen

"Thanks, I need all the prayers I can get because I can't stop thinking about her day or night," Bud said wiping the moisture from his brow.

"I could ask Betty if she has talked to her lately, maybe she could shed some light on the subject," Jack offered to help Bud.

"No, don't do that, she needs to decide this on her own and I don't want her knowing what effect it is having on me, that will give her more reason to torment me. Remember Jack, she has always been somewhat of a tease."

"Yes, she gave you a hard time…remember the time shortly before we graduated, she went out with another guy after the football game and you couldn't find her anywhere and when you found her she was at the drug store having a soda with the guy. I thought then she was mean spirited and Bud maybe she hasn't changed and you could be better off without her in your life."

"You may be right, but how do I move on from here?"

"Just like you did before when you came back and she was married."

"I just wish I knew why she looked me up, why now?"

After Bud left Jack and Krista sat quietly listening to the sounds of creaking floors, people walking, doors shutting and water running. The Inn was full of strangers from all lifestyles and all corners of the world. Jack took Krista's hand in his and giving it a little squeeze told her how proud he was of her tenacity and determination to have everything just so and that it was paying off with more reservations for the coming months. She gleamed with delight thanking him for all the work he had done.

"I couldn't have done this without you, Jack, you were the one that made my dreams come true and I'm so grateful." She said kissing him and snuggling up close to him as he put his arm around her shoulder pulling her to him. "And the Schmidts were wonderful. How fortunate we were to have them here to help and I believe they enjoyed every minute."

"Sometimes it is easier working for someone else — not as much responsibility."

"You're probably right. They didn't have the worries they used to, just the fun part of running an inn. It was helpful having Bud here to do some of the heavy lifting. But, those girls, Sandy and Ginny, they were priceless. Ginny was getting a kick out of the whole thing. I heard her tell her mom how romantic it was and this is where she wants to spend her honeymoon. Her mom said, 'Not anytime soon I hope,' then Ginny said, 'Oh mom.' it reminded me of how Betty and my mom were," turning to Krista, he said. "So, now, maybe we can start talking about the future, our future. Like where are we going to live?"

"Oh Jack, we have to live here at the Inn, it would just be too hard to live away from here. Don't you think?" Krista said not wanting to appear pushy but still lending rationality to the situation.

"I don't want to sell my place and I'm not too keen on renting it out to strangers and what about your cabin. We will be like rich people with a winter place, a summer place, and a weekend place. It doesn't make much sense."

"Jack, we don't have to decide tonight, we just need to think it through and I'm sure we will come up with a great solution to our dilemma," Krista assured him.

"You're right, we will work it out together," Jack told her looking into the angelic expression on her face, knowing without a doubt in his mind that he would be living with her here at the Inn and for some reason, he felt good about it.

Chapter **13**

The welcome buds of spring covered the rose bushes in the garden, the ground held a carpet of purple clover and daffodils popped up everywhere while the wormy nastiness from the Oak trees covered everything with yellow pollen. Krista kept a constant vigil with the broom and garden hose. She made sure the guests were not inconvenienced by the layers of yellow mist that attaches itself to anything in its way, as if it could propagate on windshields and lawn furniture.

After a morning of tending to her chores around the Inn, she was off to purchase supplies for the next few days. She was finally out of the boot even though she could not wear any of her regular shoes. But she was relieved to be able to drive again. Her first stop was the Bakery downtown where she found they made excellent sweet rolls, better than her own. She bought some for breakfast the next day, then it was off to the health food store for honey and jam. She found it harder these days, with less time, to make her scones daily, so she saved them for special treats to her guests on Saturdays.

At her final stop, the local food market, she gathered items for her own shelves and more necessities for the Inn. Rounding the corner with her cart, she nearly ran over Mrs. Schmidt or Elsa as she finally convinced Krista they were good enough friends that she could call them by their first names Elsa and Herman.

"My goodness, where are you going in such a hurry, dear?"

"Oh I'm sorry, I was not paying attention, this is my last stop and I need to get home soon because I have some newlyweds checking in this afternoon," she said leading the way to the cash register.

"How's the new girl working out?"

"Thank you so much, Elsa, for sending her to me, she is a jewel, a hard worker and it has helped so much."

"You enjoy the Inn, don't you dear?"

"Yes, I do, it is a happy place that makes me happy."

"I'm so glad and we are so happy for you and Jack, what a perfect union. How are the wedding plans going?"

"Actually, pretty well, I've ordered the dresses and the invitations," Krista said, putting her items on the conveyor belt and watching the figures coming up on the screen. "I think you rang that one twice," she said to the cashier.

The cashier checked the tape and removed the second ring then while Krista kept a close eye on items, she listened to Elsa tell about Herman's doctor appointment. "Well, that is good news. I'm sure that is a relief to both of you," Krista said knowing how concerned Elsa had been about Herman's health. "We haven't been to lunch in a while Elsa. Let's do something about that, say Thursday," Elsa agreed and Krista followed the package guy through the doors.

Without a word from her, he went straight to her car, she clicked the opener and he put her purchases in the back seat. Before she could thank him, he headed back to the store pushing her cart. She got in the car and put the key in the ignition but hesitated. *I've seen him somewhere before, but where?* She thought, then pulled out onto the highway thinking about the many things she needed to do as her thoughts went in a completely different direction.

*****

"I saw Elsa at the store today, Herman seems to be fine after seeing the doctor. I hope it won't be too much for them to watch the Inn for us while we are gone."

"We won't be so far away that we can't come back if they need us. Branson is only a few minutes away, remember we sorta planned it that way if I recall," Jack said with a chuckle.

"A certain someone we know didn't want to be that far from her 'baby'."

"Now Jack, you know this is a business and it will be the busy time of the season. Maybe we should put off the honeymoon until winter. We could close down and head for the tropics," she answered pleading with him.

"I think we had this discussion here a while back and decided to go to Branson for three days, not a month but three days."

"I know, but we could stay here at the Crescent Hotel for our wedding night then go someplace wonderful next year."

"You know what little lady, you're stubborn, but I'm beginning to see your reasoning," he said putting his arms around her waist and pulling her next to him. "As long as we get married as planned then I'm okay with waiting until winter for the honeymoon. But I get to pick the place, deal?"

"Deal! Thank you, Jack."

"Well, I better head for the 'Ranch', I miss being here with you."

"I know I miss you too, but Jack you have so much to do at your place and I have kept you here taking care of me long enough. I'll see you in the morning. Besides, 'absence makes the heart grow fonder', or that's what they say."

"Well, I don't know who 'they' are but my heart grows fonder of you every day and I can't wait to live with you like your husband as well as your caregiver whenever needed."

She watched as he drove away waving back to her. She sat down in the swing on the porch with Goldie by her side. "Well, girl this has been a wild few months." Goldie lifted her chin from the wooden planks on the floor as her big brown eyes looked up at her master as if in agreement. Krista went over in her mind, the events of the last few months. Deep in thought, she was unaware of anyone around. Suddenly Goldie growled bringing Krista out of her thoughts. Just then the man she had seen take out her groceries ran past the porch. Goldie came to her feet as Krista told her to stay. Then she stepped off the porch and called after the man, but he kept running then he turned and went down between the buildings and disappeared.

She wondered if he could be the same man she saw that cold snowy day looking in the window, the one she had seen running at night along this road and the same one lurking in the shadows across the street. She ran back in the building and down the stairs to the other street below hoping to get a glimpse of him maybe across the street and sure enough, there he was, running up the hill across from the Inn. She stepped out on the sidewalk and called to him again. This time he slowed down, turned around and looked at her while walking backward. She shouted loud enough for him to hear and she thought he was going to come back but then he was at the intersection at the top of the hill and he turned again and disappeared.

Molly Owen

She went back inside and turned the closed sign around making sure the instruction to ring the buzzer for help after hours was showing. Still a little unnerved that the man would not come and talk to her, she made her way back up the stairs, a little slower now because her ankle was aching. She scolded herself for running down the stairs. When she got to her kitchen, she pulled out a tray of ice and with a tea towel made an ice pack for her ankle. Back to the couch where she had spent weeks, she propped her foot up and applied the ice. The sun was down behind the mountain now and darkness filled the neighborhood as streetlights came on. Goldie whined and nudged Krista's hand. "Sorry Girl, I didn't let you go down the stairs but I didn't want you to trip me. You're a good girl Goldie," she said, patting her on the head. Her ankle was hurting more now and she decided to take some of the medicine she had for pain.

The phone kept ringing until Krista came out of a pill-induced sleep. She reached for the phone and answered it.

"Hello"

"Krista, are you okay? You sound funny, were you asleep? It's only nine o'clock. I told you not to do so much too soon." Jack scolded

"I know."

"What's going on Krista? You sound like you did when you were taking those painkillers. Is your ankle hurting?"

She sat up and found her head swimming, then remembered she had not eaten anything. *This is not good.* She told herself lying back down. She heard Jack calling her through the phone. Then she heard him say he was on his way.

The next thing she knew he was in her living room standing over her and asking her what happened to her visibly swollen ankle. Before she could answer, he went to the kitchen to put on some water for tea and make another ice pack. Then he asked her if she had eaten and she said no so he began to make her a sandwich.

"I'm so sorry Jack….I know I shouldn't have done it…I just wasn't thinking. I just wanted to talk to him."

"Him? Him who?" Jack said frustrated.

"The man that was at the window, in the shadow across the street, the man that carried my groceries to the car today, the same man I have seen running in front of my home….that's who," Krista said almost crying.

"I'm sorry Krista, I shouldn't have questioned you…it's just that I'm so terribly worried about you….can you understand…I love you and I don't want anything to happen to you….why did you run after him? He could have hurt you."

"I don't think he's dangerous…he stopped running and turned around when he heard me call out to him but then he went on. If he wanted to hurt me he had plenty of opportunities."

Molly Owen

"Okay, tell me again how this happened and don't leave anything out."

Krista put the half-eaten sandwich down, adjusted the ice pack, and told Jack the whole event again trying to remember everything including hurting her ankle and putting the ice pack on and taking the pill on an empty stomach. "And then you came and I'm sorry you're so worried about me. I think it is a withdrawal on your part. Because you got so used to taking care of me you think I can't take care of myself."

"So Goldie, do you think I can trust her to take care of herself?"

Goldie whined and laid down beside Krista. Jack sat very still for a minute looking at Krista. She watched him, wondering what was going through his mind. She did not blame him for being upset with her, truth be known, she was upset with herself. She was worried that her ankle could be damaged, all because she forgot to be careful and not run down the stairs.

Jack got up from the chair and walked over to the couch, lifted her foot, and put it on the coffee table, then sitting down beside her, put his arm around her. "Forgive me, Krista."

"Forgive me! I'm the one who acted foolishly. I don't blame you for being upset."

Bowing his head, Jack thanked God for keeping Krista safe and asked Him to heal her ankle. "In Jesus' Name. Amen"

"Amen."

"I'll stay here tonight and take you to the doctor in the morning."

"Are you mad at me, Jack?"

"No, disappointed, but I'm not mad."

"Because I wasn't careful or is it something else?"

"Now that you ask, I'm wondering where you got the painkillers, I thought you were out."

"I was but I refilled the prescription, and I guess it was a good thing I did because I needed a painkiller. Why? What are you saying, Jack? Do you think I have been taking them all along? Go look at the bottle," Krista said seeing the doubt on his face

Jack went to the cabinet in the kitchen where she kept the medicine and took the bottle out. The date on the bottle was soon after she took the last of the other bottle.

"Go ahead, count them," Krista said irritated.

"Krista, please understand, it is so easy to get hooked on painkillers, I have seen many grown men in the military get hooked and I just don't want that to happen to you."

"Count them, Jack, you need to believe me but you won't until you count them. The one I took tonight was the only one I've taken since I filled the prescription. Go ahead, you'll see."

He wanted so desperately to believe her but he knew she was right, until he counted the pills he could not be sure and he needed to be sure. He poured the pills onto a plate and began to count them. There were exactly 29 pills in the bottle. He took a deep breath and turned to find Krista crying. When he approached her, she pushed him away.

"Please leave, Jack. Just leave," she said between sobs.

Jack realized she was in no mood to listen to him as much as he protested, so he left feeling so guilty that he felt like someone had died. The feeling was nearly unbearable as he drove down the street from her not wanting to leave her alone. He wished he had taken the pills with him. *What am I saying? She would never do anything rash? Would she?* He stopped the car at the end of the street contemplating whether to go back or not.

A man stood on the sidewalk just feet from his truck. He stared into his bearded face. The man stared back at him as he stood like a statue.

Jack opened the door to his truck and stepped down onto the street. He left the lights on so he could see better. Walking around the front of the truck, he walked toward the figure under the streetlight.

"Mason, is that you?"

"One in the same brother…"

"I almost didn't recognize you under that growth on your face."

"It helps keep me warm."

"Jack what's going on?" a voice behind him said. As he turned, he saw Bud coming up beside the truck.

"How did you get here? Where did you come from?"

"I just came by to visit when I saw your truck and saw you were talking to this man and thought I should check it out. Who is this guy anyway?"

"Well, the last time I saw him he was a boy and now he's all grown up and sporting a beard. Bud, do you remember my little brother, Mason?"

"No! Mason? I would have never known you if I saw you on the street." Bud said, offering his hand for a shake.

"This is the man that Krista has been seeing and the one she saw in the window," Jack said.

"So you must be the one that called the night Krista got hurt."

"Yeah, after he caused her to fall in the first place," Jack said. "Do you have any idea how much pain you inflicted on her, not only that night, but tonight too. She injured her ankle again chasing after you."

"Is she okay?" Bud said.

"I don't know, I'm taking her to the doctor in the morning if she will let me," Jack said.

Molly Owen

Torn between two opposite emotions, on one hand, relief not only at seeing his brother after all the years but also that he finally knew the identity of the mystery man. On the other hand, his anger at his little brother for all the anguish he brought to bear, not only on Krista, but also on himself and his sister who thought of him often and wondered what had happened to him. He was not quite sure how to handle the situation, since he knew he had deeply offended Krista just minutes before, but he needed her to know who this man turned out to be. He had so many questions and wanted the answers soon.

"Krista's pretty upset with me right now and she hurt her ankle again. Would you mind staying with her while I sort things out with Mason?"

"Sure, I'll leave you two to catch up," Bud said, then he went back to Krista's to check on her ankle.

Jack told Mason to get in the truck. Shutting the door, he reached down to start the engine but stopped and turned to Mason. "Where are you staying?"

"Nowhere and everywhere, there are many places to hide around here in abandoned buildings, caves, under bridges, you name it, I've stayed there."

"Don't you have a job? Krista saw you at the grocery store, she said you bagged her groceries."

"That barely pays enough to buy food, let alone a place to sleep. You know how I knew you lived here in Eureka Springs?"

"No, how?"

"Remember last fall when you came home and saw someone run into the woods? That was me, I just wanted some food but I didn't know it was your place until I saw you in your headlights."

"Why didn't you show yourself, let me know it was you?" Jack asked, frustrated at his brother's lack of sense.

"I don't know, I guess I was afraid," Mason said looking down at the hands in his lap. He kept twisting them then one finger at a time he would pop a knuckle. This was exactly the reason he did not want Jack to know who he was. He knew he would grill him with questions and he did not want to answer them. He did not want big brother to know what a failure he was and how he lived on the streets and barely had enough money to eat.

When he left this part of the world his plan was to go out and make it big and then come back a success, so Jack and Betty would be proud of him, but it hadn't worked out that way at all. His life had been one mistake after another for the past ten years. So, he had come back to the Ozarks hoping to find work so he could again be part of his family. Seeing Jack that night had been a stroke of luck, or so he thought, until he went into town and saw him working at the Inn. He did not want to horn in on anything Jack had going, then there was Krista. He wondered about Debbie but soon realized she was no longer in the picture.

"Jack what happened between you and Debbie, I thought you two would get married someday."

"We did get married. She died of breast cancer over six years ago."

"Oh, sorry, I didn't know," Mason said, "and Betty?"

"She and Ben have three kids and still live in Berryville."

After sitting in the truck for a long while, Jack decided to take Mason to McDonald's and feed him while he thought about what to do about Krista. He looked back and was glad to see that Bud was still with Krista. He called him on his cell and told him where he and Mason were going and asked if he could stay with Krista until he got back.

After they had dinner at McDonald's, Jack took Mason out to his place and told him to make himself at home, then went back to Krista's. When he arrived, Krista was in bed asleep and Bud was sitting watching TV.

"Boy, you have such an exciting life, Jack." Bud teased.

"Yeah, really exciting and complicated, I guess Mason can stay with me awhile. I don't know what to make of him, all these months and not letting me know he was here and stalking us like we were against him somehow. He hasn't told me everything that's for sure. He may never tell me everything. How's Krista doing?"

"Well, I think she understands what was going through your head tonight, but bro you were pretty rough on her. Did you think she was addicted to the pills?"

"I didn't know what to think, she was pretty much out of it when I got here and I didn't know she had refilled her prescription. Anyway, I hope she forgives me."

"I kind of filled her in on some stuff, so I think she will forgive you," Bud said, getting up and heading for the door.

"Thanks, Bud, for staying, I'll stay here and get her to the doctor in the morning."

"Good idea, but I think she will be okay, the swelling has gone down and she didn't take another pill before she went to bed. She may have just strained the muscles in her ankle. See ya."

Chapter **14**

After reconciling their differences over breakfast, Jack tried to explain Mason's actions without much success. Krista wondered what would happen now that he was back in Jack's life. They went to the doctor and after an X-ray to make sure there was no damage, they went to Sparkie's for lunch. Jack, still unnerved by the events of the night before, remained quiet as they ate their meal. There seemed to be some strain between them for the first time in their relationship. *Was it Mason? Was it the pill thing?* He wasn't sure but something was not right.

"Are you okay," he asked.

"Sure, are you? You've been awfully quiet,"

"Just trying to figure out what to do with Mason, he's working part-time at the grocery store but he says he isn't making enough money to feed himself let alone pay rent. I don't know how he expects to get a job with that mountain man beard. That's the first thing he needs to do to get a decent job and maybe I can get him some clothes, he looks so thin I'm sure he won't be able to wear my clothes, so I'll need to buy some for him. I can't believe he has been in town through the coldest winter on record, sleeping on the street, basically. I just don't understand what has happened to him."

Jack noticed that Krista was not saying anything, pro or con, which made him wonder if she was having second thoughts about the wedding and at this point, he would not blame her. The last few hours had been difficult on more levels than one and he didn't know how to fix it. At the end of their meal, he went to pay while she walked outside to wait on him. He opened the door to the truck and helped her step in then shut the door. Back behind the wheel before turning the key, he looked at her. She was looking straight ahead and did not turn to look at him.

"Krista, what is it, why are you ignoring me? I thought we had straightened things out between us. Are you still upset with me?" he asked, almost afraid of the answer.

"I was just wondering if Mason's return is going to interfere with our wedding plans. You seem to be so concerned about him, as you should be, but maybe we need to postpone our wedding until, I don't know, the fall maybe. That would give him time to settle in, to get a job, a place to live, reunite with the family," Krista said, still looking straight ahead.

"Krista, look at me, is that the only reason you want to postpone the wedding, because of Mason?" he said with his hand under her chin turning her face toward him.

"I'm just confused right now, we have never had a serious disagreement in all these months, working side by side and now I can't shake this feeling, you said that you were disappointed in me without trusting me. Isn't that what marriage is all about, trust?" she said tears rolling down her cheeks onto his hand still on her chin.

Taking his hand away, he handed her his handkerchief. What was he going to do to convince her he was wrong and he did trust her after the way he acted? He sat with his head down saying a silent prayer. *God, please help me to say the right thing.*

"Krista, I love you more than life itself. I do trust you. Sometimes I think I love you too much. I want our lives together to be perfect and I know that can't happen because we are human, we make mistakes. Even if you had become addicted to the pain pills I would have stood by your side and done everything in my power to help you. I made a mistake. I'm sorry. I'm asking you to forgive me for my mistake and let's learn from it. We know how hurtful it is and we should be able to avoid this sort of misunderstanding in the future. Last night was unfortunate and I can't promise we will never face something like that again in the future. I love you, Krista, I want you to be my wife," he said his own tears pooling in his eyelids ready to spill over.

Molly Owen

Krista leaned over and put her arms around his neck. "I love you too Jack, I love you so much and I can't imagine life without you."

"Do you forgive me?

"Yes, I forgive you," she said, pulling away from him long enough to receive his kiss.

"Let's pray," he said with his arms still holding her.

"Father, we praise you, You are the almighty and worthy of our praise. Thank you for our forgiveness to each other, Lord, Jesus. We ask Your blessing on this union. Help us be kind, thoughtful, and understanding with each other by keeping You at the center of our relationship. We pray this in Your name, Jesus. Amen."

*****

Back at the Inn, they relieved Sarah, who had held down the fort while they had gone to the doctor and lunch.

"Thank you, Sarah, we can take over now, we appreciate you filling in for us," Jack told her.

"How's your ankle, Krista?"

"It's fine, just sore, thanks for asking," Krista told Sarah, hoping she did not notice the lack of makeup wiped from her face earlier.

Sarah left through the store's door to her car parked on the street. Krista asked Jack to leave her alone in the store for a while so she could straighten up a little and restock the shelves. Truth be known, she wanted some time alone because she had some thinking to do. Even though they had not made a decision about where to live, she had been thinking it was time to sell the cabin. It was part of her past, and she needed to let go of it. She wasn't sure how Jack would feel about it. It would need some repairs before she could sell it and maybe Mason could help with that. He could stay there while he worked on it and Jack could go over and check on things. Then she realized that neither she nor Jack knew at this time what Mason's skills were, however, she was sure Jack could teach him what he needed to know. She wondered if trust was an issue with Jack remembering Bud's talk with her about Mason.

An only child, and not especially close to Drew's siblings gave her little experience with brothers and sisters. She wondered how Betty would feel about Mason after all this time. She also wondered if Mason's issues were still a major part of him as in the past. Bud told her Mason had been in real trouble before leaving Berryville, although he was never sentenced to jail he had spent some time there as a teenager. He never finished high school and that was probably the reason for his lack of a good job. Krista wondered how much he would resist Jack's offer to help him. Cutting his hair and shaving his beard would probably be the hardest thing to convince him to do.

Molly Owen

A couple of hours passed before Jack returned to the Inn after taking Mason to work at the grocery store. He came down the stairs with a large bouquet of roses he got at the florist up the street. Keeping them behind his back he leaned over the counter and gave her a kiss then produced the roses. Handing them to her, he said, "I love you, sweetheart."

"How sweet, thank you Jack, but you didn't need to," she said putting her nose to the roses. "They smell so good."

"Are you ready to go upstairs, I thought I would cook outside and we could sit on the porch? At least we won't have to worry about that stranger showing up unannounced," he said with a smile.

Sitting on the porch with Goldie at their feet, they watched in silence as the sun went down casting shadows over the area. Jack had gone down to answer the buzzer and let a couple into the Inn but soon returned.

"Are they a nice young couple?"

"Actually they are older, I'd say in their fifties."

"Romance is still blooming all over the Inn and I love it," she said with excitement in her voice. "Jack tell me about your friend Ernie."

"What about him? That was quite a switch from Romance to Tragedy. I'm sure Bud told you about it."

"He skimmed the top but didn't fill in many details."

"The three musketeers, that's what everyone called us. All through school, we hung out together. Ernie had a hard family life and we tried to keep him on the straight and narrow. His family was not believers and even though we tried, he would not attend church with us. Then one summer in high school, Bud and I were going to work as counselors at our church camp. We invited Ernie to come along, he hesitated at first but then decided to go. Bud and I hadn't seen much of him since the school was out for the summer so we thought this would be fun to have the three of us together.

"Anyway, we were going on one of the trails above the caves and he slipped and fell about thirty feet breaking his hip, leg, and arm. He was in the hospital for several weeks then rehab but the accident left him with a noticeable limp. We went to see him all the time and when he got out of the hospital, he went home. However, he didn't want us to come to his house. I guess he was embarrassed about his family.

"We didn't see him the next year and heard he wasn't coming back to school. Right after we graduated, we saw him one day at the drug store where we all hung out and he was wasted. He could hardly stand upright. We took him home and left him on his porch. The rumor was that he was addicted to the painkillers. Later he was arrested for stealing drugs from the local pharmacist. After Bud and I joined the army, he got out of jail and back to his old habits. Then one day I got a letter from Betty, she told me he committed suicide. I felt bad, it just seemed like we could have done more and for a long time I felt guilty about him falling and his addiction and even his suicide."

"But it wasn't your fault Jack, he made his own choices."

"I know, but I have been acutely aware of addictions ever since. I was even worried about Debbie when she was on painkillers and she was not going to get better and needed them, that's how irrational I am about addictions."

"Are you worried about Mason?"

"Yes, although there is not an indication that he has any kind of addiction. He doesn't smoke, drink beer, and as far as I know, doesn't even take over-the-counter medicines."

Krista decided to talk to Jack later about her cabin idea hoping it would somehow relieve his mind where Mason was concerned.

Chapter *15*

Tourists flocked the area as the busiest season of the year got into full swing with school out for the summer and warm weather, families came out for the fun-filled activities in and around Eureka Springs. Working hard every day gave little occasion for any private time as the Inn was full nearly every night and the store was flourishing much to Krista's delight. Vendors were also pleased with the stream of orders, as stocking the store was a constant while people shopped for weddings, birthdays, and even next year's Christmas gifts. Because of the success of the Inn, a tearoom opened close by bringing more people to the shop, and then reservations increased for the Inn. Krista was beginning to be concerned that she and Jack would be unable to have even one night for a honeymoon as busy as they stayed. Because Krista's ankle had healed enough for her to wear normal shoes they decided to go on with the date on the invitations she had ordered weeks ago.

*****

Jack was not sure about selling the cabin but they took Mason out to see it and were delighted when he actually came up with the idea of clearing some of the dead trees, repairing the dock, fixing the storage shed, and painting inside and out. They reached an agreement and Jack spent every other day going to the cabin to make sure everything was being done. sometimes he would help Mason with the two-man jobs.

Watching Mason at work, Jack noted that his little brother had picked up some skills over the years. He was a master at carpentry and knew his way around the toolbox. There were a few things Jack gave him some tips on that made the job easier or faster but overall he trusted Mason to do the job right.

One afternoon Jack arrived to find his brother more recognizable. His clean-shaven face took years off and he looked more his age.

"I like it, Mason, you look like I remember you when you were younger. Why now? You got a girl out here I don't know about."

"No, you know I wouldn't do that after all you have done for me."

"I was kidding Mason I didn't mean I thought you had a girl out here, I was just surprised that you suddenly decided to shave it all off."

"Oh," Mason said, a little embarrassed.

"How's it going, anyway? Looks like you've gotten a lot accomplished in the last couple of days. I think this place will be ready to put on the market real soon."

"I wanted to talk to you about that. Do you think Krista would mind if I stayed out here while she tried to sell the place? I know she is listing it with Sandy and I would be glad to show it and it would probably be smart to have someone living here, don't you think?"

"Yes, you're probably right. I'll ask Krista. Are you sure you want to stay out here by yourself? Don't you get lonely?"

"No, I love it out here. It is really peaceful, nobody bothers me and I can just be myself," Mason said looking out over the cove. "I go fishing nearly every day and watch the deer come back and forth through the property. It's nice, you know?"

Jack looked at Mason and wondered how long had it been since he had a real bed, a place to call home?

That evening after they closed the shop they decided to go to the Crescent for dinner. It was a beautiful evening with temperatures around eighty and a slight breeze keeping the heat of the day at bay. Jack forwarded the Inn phone number to his cell then taking Krista's arm, he led her to the truck. Walking into the restaurant they waved at the owner then followed the waiter to a table by the window. Even though they had the menu memorized, they looked anyway. After they ordered and the waiter poured their wine, they began to relax. Jack put a lot of thought into what he was about to propose to Krista while driving back to Eureka Springs from the cabin.

Taking the white cloth napkin from the table in front of her, Krista, unfolded it and laid it across her lap. Raising the stemmed glass to her lips, she sipped the wine, put it down then took a deep breath. Since Sarah had a spring cold and stayed home for the day she had had a very busy day checking in guests, running the store and restocking soap, towels, chocolates, and flowers. Relaxing over a nice dinner with Jack was just what she needed. Not noticing his preoccupation she began to tell him about her day and how she didn't think she could run things alone tomorrow if Sarah stayed home another day.

"How are things at the cabin? Will you be able to help me? I know you want to check on Mason but I need you here and he seems to be doing so well, you said so yourself, he has many of the same skills you have. What do you think? Can you stay in town and help tomorrow?"

"Actually, Mason came up with a plan he wanted me to talk to you about," Jack said. After explaining and bragging about the fact that he had shaved his beard and trimmed his hair, he went on to say, "I think he enjoys living out there where he's his own man, so to speak. I realize he's still dependent but I get the idea that he hasn't slept in a real bed or had a roof over his head for quite a while and you should see how clean he keeps the place like he's proud of it. Perhaps he could offer his services to some of the neighbors out there you know, some of the same things he has been doing, that would give him some income. As time went on he could buy a car and come into Garfield and work then he would be self-sufficient. In the meantime, he would take care of the cabin. We don't need to sell it right away and it would give him the chance to be a human again. You should have seen the look on his face when he was talking to me about it. It was like a dream come true."

"So are you saying we wouldn't sell the cabin, just let Mason live there until he was back on his feet," Krista said.

"It is up to you Krista, I don't want you to do anything you're uncomfortable with," Jack said, not sure how she was reacting to his suggestion.

"Well, it is kind of sudden, I thought we had a plan, but let me think about it and we'll talk again, okay? I just want to relax without anything important to think about right now."

"Sure, it's just an idea, don't fret about it. If you don't think it will work then please just tell me that, it won't hurt my feelings at all. I just want you to be happy with any decision we make."

Reaching across the table, she took his hand and told him she loved him and they would talk about it later. "I know you want what's best for your brother and so do I. We have so many things to decide very soon, however, right now I just want to clear my head and spend a romantic dinner with the love of my life."

Squeezing her hand, he gave her a wink, put his napkin in his lap just in time for the waiter to set their food in front of them. Holding hands, he thanked God for His grace and asked Him to bless their food. Raising their heads, the conversation went to wedding plans while enjoying the wonderful cuisine, down to the chocolate soufflé topped with whipped cream and served in a tall stemmed goblet. After dinner, they walked hand in hand through the beautiful flower gardens, watching several squirrels scamper up and down trees and a jackrabbit nibbling on some greens. Arriving back at Krista's sedan, Jack opened the door after kissing her. Then like a teenager ran around to the driver's side and as soon as he got in, he leaned over and stole one more kiss before starting the car and driving away.

Krista knew her only hesitation about Mason staying at the cabin, if she were honest, maybe not the only hesitation, Sandy would not get the listing. Right now, it was the only justification she could find for her misgivings because if she admitted to herself, the real reason went much deeper than that, she was ready to let go of Drew and keeping the cabin would not allow that and she was looking forward to moving on with a new beginning.

She remembered early in their relationship, Jack telling her how he had moved on after Debbie's death, moved to Eureka Springs and built the cabin he now lived in, so perhaps he would understand her reservations. The last thing she wanted was for

Jack to think it had anything to do with her feelings about Mason other than they would be more likely to go to the cabin if Mason lived there. Happy that Sandy had already sold the house in Rogers and the closing was in less than two weeks, she looked forward to putting her previous life behind her so she could move on. *Maybe that is what Jack wants for Mason, so he can put his past behind him, start over, be someone different, even happy* and it did seem like a good solution to the situation.

*****

Jack was not sure what Krista thought of the idea but he thought it was a good one considering Mason had to be somewhere, either Jack's own place, her cabin, or heaven forbid back out on the street because there was no way he could live with them. All the way home, after dropping Krista off, he had pondered the many scenarios with that one at the top of the list. Mason had proven he was a good worker and he needed a place to stay so what was the problem. Pulling into his driveway, he sat a moment watching the fireflies dance in front of the truck remembering the night he almost caught Mason coming out of his house. *If he had seen me that night, would it have changed things, would our future be different somehow?* Afraid to go there in his mind he shook off the feeling and went in through the porch to the kitchen. Coming back on the porch with a cola, he sat on the swing. *I wonder if Krista would consider living out here.*

Chapter *16*

Humidity was nearly unbearable as the heat of summer set in bringing with it the wonderful world of insects. Mason scraped the chips of paint from the siding on the storage shed while sweat dripped from his forehead, he reached for the thermos, he had found in the cupboard and took a drink of ice tea. Wiping his forehead with a handkerchief he found among items in a drawer, he stood to survey the area around him. He was so glad Krista decided to let him stay in the cabin, it made him feel normal for the first time in a long time. Since the cabin was part of Krista's past, he had to accept the fact that he could not be there forever. Swatting at a mosquito, he vowed to get some bug spray when he went to the store in Gateway.

The walk to the store was all downhill full of curves on an unpaved road, dirt stuck to the sweat, crept into his shoes, and caked in his hat. The wind had picked up about a half-mile into his walk and it looked like a storm was brewing in the distance. Hurrying to beat the rain, he stumbled on a groove in the dirt road and found himself tumbling down an incline into a ravine landing hard on a pile of rocks, he let out a scream. As if in answer to his cry, lightning streaked across the sky followed closely by a loud clap of thunder that vibrated within him.

The heavens opened with vengeance and sheets of rain poured over him taking his mind off his pain. Flashes of memories filled his head as he remembered the day his father lay drowning in the water at the bottom of a ditch trapped under his tractor. Then he remembered seeing Krista fall and hearing her cries of pain. His head began to swim as he desperately tried to stay awake.

Warmth covered his face encouraging him to open his eyes one at a time until he could see between the leaves in the trees at the sunbeams. Slowly he stretched each muscle, checking to see if he could move when suddenly the pain came and he saw blood in the water beneath him. Reaching in his pocket, he pulled out the wet handkerchief and wrapped it tightly around his head. When the bleeding didn't stop he took the material off and folded it into a square, then after tearing his shirt he replaced the square onto the wound on his forehead and wrapped the shirt material tightly around his head. Satisfied that the bleeding had stopped he assessed the situation he found himself. The mud made it hard to stand but after some attempts, he managed to pull on a root until he was climbing up the side of the ravine.

After what seemed hours, he reached the road now full of water puddles. *Oh well*, he thought, *I'm soaked anyway. What is a little more water?* He sloshed down the road finally reaching the store. After explaining his appearance, the owner helped bandage his head and gave him the key to the restroom to freshen up.

On his way back into the store, he noticed a sign hanging on the wall next to the soda machine.

"Is it okay if I take this sign with me?"

"Sure, they will put another one up."

"Thanks, see you later," Mason said stuffing the paper into the bag of supplies.

The next morning Mason sipped on his second cup of coffee as he watched the sun come up over the lake. Not being able to sleep the night before, he was up early to fix his breakfast. Remembering the events of the day before, he looked again at the paper from the store. He had not been in church since he left home. It occurred to him that having a relationship with God could have helped him through the years when he felt lost, out of control, and very much alone. Lying in the ravine remembering his father and Krista, he cried out to God for the first time since his father died. That day was when he pleaded with God for it not to be true that his Dad was dead. Every

Sunday he sat in church with his mother and siblings but he didn't feel that God cared about him.

When his mother died, he knew God did not care about him and that's when he went on his way. The next few years were very hard, he missed his family, his home, and something else was missing, too, that he could not put his finger on. However, yesterday he realized that not having God in his life had brought him nothing but grief. He watched Jack and Krista, how happy they were, and knew they were close to God. Betty and Ben were also Christians and raising their family with Christ the center of their lives.

It was Sunday and Mason decided to follow the urging of the message on the paper and attend a church meeting up on Whitney Mountain. He put on a clean pair of Jeans and a freshly ironed shirt then began the mile walk to the church with the bible he found in the nightstand by his bed.

The temperature was rising and along with the moisture from the rain the day before, it was becoming sticky as Mason tried not to hurry so he would not be dripping in sweat when he arrived but to no avail, he began to wipe his face. The building came into view and he began to straighten his clothes as he approached the door, pausing as he went in and when no one turned to see who entered he sat at the very back away from others.

The cool air inside the church was welcomed and soon he began to relax as he listened intently to the message on John 3:16 by the pastor. Verses from the bible began to return as he remembered the teaching from his childhood and opened the bible in his hand. Surprised that he still remembered the books of the bible, he turned to the third chapter of John and began to read along with the others. Not wanting to go through the greeting process, Mason left during the closing prayer. He hurried down the road then took a shortcut on the way back to the cabin.

Thoughts of the past, present, and future flooded his mind as he cut through the woods to the cabin. It seemed to Mason that sin had become his middle name. He desperately wanted to start his life over, on a new track that included God Almighty if He would have him. He recalled the cross, and the meaning of it all came back to him. Suddenly he fell to his knees and prayed aloud, loud and clear.

"God, forgive me, give me the Grace promised."

As his words rang out throughout the land, he began to feel peace for the first time in years.

"Mason? Who are you talking to?"

Mason turned to see Jack standing on the hill behind him. He slumped with his head on his chest.

"Mason, are you all right?" Jack said stumbling down the hill grabbing tree limbs to steady himself until he was a few feet from Mason.

"Yes, Jack for the first time in a very long time I'm going to be alright with the help of God, I'm going to have a future," Mason said with tears running down his face.

"What happened, I mean why out here?"

"I went to church this morning, I have been thinking about it for weeks and then I saw a sign in the store yesterday for this church and I went. I fell down a ravine yesterday and hit my head on a rock," he said, putting his hand on the wound on his forehead. "Well, while I laid there in the water I thought about Dad and how he died and how I couldn't handle it at the time, seeing Mom all torn up. Then I started having flashbacks of Krista falling and how I felt so bad about it. That has been the story of my life feeling bad about things. Jack, I just wanted to feel good about something, like living in this cabin, working with my hands but I want more and I know what's been missing is a relationship with God."

Without a word, Jack fell on his knees next to his brother and wrapped his arms around him, and then he asked Mason if he could say a prayer. *"Father in heaven You are an awesome God. Thank you for bringing Mason back to us. Thank you for your grace through Jesus Christ, your son. Be with Mason as he renews his relationship with you. In Jesus' name, we pray Amen."* After Jack finished the prayer, he stood up and offered Mason a hand. They walked side-by-side back to the cabin. Sitting on the deck, Mason asked Jack why he was not in church.

"I was but I told Krista I had to come to see you, it was a God thing, I think."

Chapter *17*

The church dining hall decorated with flowers, bows, and ribbons surrounding swags of ivory lace draped on the serving table and tiers of plates holding cookies, cupcakes and strawberries sat in the center flanked by stacks of gifts waiting for the guest of honor. Another table held the punch bowl and urns filled with ice tea and lemonade. Anxious guests waited for the bride-to-be's arrival, cameras ready. Led by Elsa Schmidt, the bridal group, Sandy, Ginny, Betty, and her daughter Cara entered the hall. Then Krista entered the room with cameras flashing.

"Oh dear, I feel like a celebrity with all this attention. It is absolutely beautiful here. Wow, who would have thought this place could be transformed into a wonderland?" Krista said.

Many of Krista's friends were present, some from the bank in Rogers where she had worked, and employees where Drew worked. Also, new friends she made in Eureka Springs including friends from church she and Jack attended surrounded her now with best wishes. She felt overwhelmed at the outpouring of love and fellowship as she took her seat at the head table.

They played the usual bridal shower games, had refreshments, and then she began to open what seemed an enormous stack of exquisitely wrapped gifts that Krista hesitated to destroy by ripping into. She began to maneuver the ribbons and bows meticulously making sure not to tear the paper. It was a personal shower so many of the items were beautiful lacy negligees and antique jewelry, silver boudoir sets, silk pillowcases, embroidered towels with monograms, and one long silk robe from Betty.

After the shower, Jack and Krista treated the wedding party to an outing at Sparkie's where the couple's romance blossomed as they spent time after choir practice learning about each other over hamburgers and fries. The gifts were carefully loaded into Krista's car and the women found seats in three different vehicles and went to meet their menfolk at the restaurant. On arrival, Jack greeted everyone and led the group into the back part of the building where the men anxiously waited. It was a wonderful evening with friends and family eating, laughing and enjoying each other's company.

Back at the Inn, Krista found it hard to come down from all the excitement as she showed some of the gifts she received to

Jack. She deliberately didn't show him the negligees. Those were a surprise for their honeymoon. Jack delighted in watching her excitement knowing how much it meant to her. After Jack left for his cabin, Krista sat in her kitchen nursing a glass of tea, thinking about the days ahead and her pending marriage to Jack. A warm feeling came over her as she realized how blessed she was. Bowing her head she thanked God for his Grace and for giving her not one love in her life but a second love that she hoped to spend the rest of her life with, she thanked him for all His blessings and for His son, her Savior, Jesus Christ. Opening her eyes, she stroked Goldie on the head and began to prepare for a good night's sleep.

Chapter *18*

Although her ankle still swelled up every now and then, Krista was finally able to wear regular shoes and started searching for the perfect pair, in the perfect color, to match the perfect wedding dress. Finally, after pouring over page after page of wedding accessories Krista was able to put together a vintage wedding including the perfect shoes for her dress and spats to go with the striped tuxedo with tails for Jack.

Sarah and Sandy's assignments were the church decorations. Krista and Betty were decorating the Crescent Hotel for the reception. In keeping with the white table and chairs in the banquet room, they put white bird cages filled with white roses topped with ecru satin bows in the center of each table. Sprays of white roses from the wedding would flank the head table.

"A vintage wedding reception in a vintage hotel, how romantic, Jack said you would come to the reception in a horse-drawn carriage," Betty said gleaming with excitement.

"Did he tell you about the night he proposed to me?

"No. I bet it was very romantic, knowing Jack."

She told Betty about that night from beginning to end including the scary trip to Springdale to be with Sandy at the hospital.

"So that is why you're having the carriage."

"Yes, Jack insisted and I'm so glad because it goes along with everything else."

That night after the rehearsal dinner at the Crescent Hotel, the wedding party went to the church. The pastor organized the affair and except for the uncertainty of the young children's roles, everything went well. Betty and her family left the church after giving Krista a hug then they headed for Jack's place. Sandy, Ginny, and Brad were staying in the Inn and Mason was staying with his family at Jack's place.

Bud, being the best man, went to the firehouse to make sure everyone knew the plans for the old fashioned English shivaree at the rented honeymoon cabin. When Bud found out where Jack and Krista would spend their wedding night he remembered reading about a custom borrowed by the English settlers from a French Charivari brought to America with early French settlers, where local boys would bang on pots and pans and serenade the couple on their first night as husband and wife.

With the permission of the property owners, friends of Jack's, Bud and his buddies planned to surround the cabin shortly after the bride and groom arrived then they would create a barrage of disturbing noise until Jack came to the door and made them leave. In the French version the local boys expected the groom to feed them a midnight supper. But Bud knew his friend would not hear of a midnight meal but they would do their best to make the shivaree a memorable occasion.

*****

"I'll see you tomorrow. I love you and can't wait until you're my wife." Jack leaned down and gave her a kiss and with a hug left her at her door.

Krista was having a hard time sleeping as she tossed and turned, listening to the sounds of the guests throughout the Inn. Usually, she slept through it, but tonight the creaking floors under the weight of footsteps and doors opening and shutting and water running through the pipes kept her aware of the activity in the old building. In a way, it was a comfort to her knowing everything was running smoothly and she could relax while she and Jack were gone. He had convinced her they could stay away from the Inn for two nights. The Schmidts would stay in one of the rooms on the first floor until they got back. Finally, her mind cleared and sleep came.

Molly Owen

"Oh, what a beautiful morning, Oh, what a beautiful day," she sang to the birds outside her window as she headed for the shower. *"Thank you, Father, for this beautiful day. Thank you for all the blessings and for Jack, oh, thank you for Jack. It's our wedding day,"* she said to her image in the mirror.

Her wedding dress was in the parlor at the church where she would get dressed. Everything else was packed and ready to go. The Schmidts would take her to the church and Herman Schmidt would give her away. They had become parents to her and she was so pleased when Herman agreed to fill the role of her father.

Again, she thanked God for the sunshine and asked His blessing on the evening wedding. She read her vows one more time before putting them in the carrying case. The sandwich she forced herself to eat earlier was sitting heavy on her stomach. Soon she was loading Schmidt's car and they were on their way. Parked behind the church was Jack's shiny new white pickup truck. Krista went in the back door making sure to avoid seeing Jack. The female part of the party was in the parlor and when Krista came through the door, the little girls squealed and ran to her giving her a hug.

Sandy was in charge of putting Krista's carrot red hair in cascades of curls. Krista had let her hair grow long. "It was easy to put back in a ponytail out of my face plus Jack likes it long," Krista told Betty's little girl when she asked her about her long red hair.

Elsa helped Krista slip her dress on and fasten the pearl buttons up the back. The ecru lace dress flowed down the curves of her body then puddled on the floor behind her. Attached to a headband, white roses and baby's breath cascaded down one side of her head allowing the lace veil to hang over her shoulders and cover her arms. Standing in front of the mirror, silence filled the room.

"You're beautiful dear, perfect in every way. Right out of one of those catalogs you have." Elsa said, choking back tears.

"Now stop that or I'll ruin my makeup if I start the waterworks."

Sandy walked up beside Krista and side by side, they looked in the mirror together. "You're beautiful, Jack will melt when he sees you."

"Amen to that," Betty said.

Elsa kissed Krista on the cheek and left the room to join her escort waiting to take her to her seat.

About that time, the music started to play and it was time to go. Sandy handed Krista her bouquet of baby's breath nestled in between budding white roses, then she and Betty left the room followed by the young girls. Herman knocked on the door.

"Come in."

Molly Owen

"I could not be more proud if you were my own daughter, Krista. Are you ready to marry that nervous man, waiting at the front of the church?" Herman asked.

"I am," she said, smiling then put her hand on his arm as they left the room.

Walking down the aisle all she could see was Jack standing in front of her and the closer she got she realized tears covered his face. After they exchanged rings, they whispered their vows to each other.

"Krista, I knew the first time I met you how special you are. I promise to honor you at all times, to love you unconditionally, and walk beside you until death do us part. You are my life."

"Jack, you brought life back to me when I was broken. My love for you is immeasurable. You are my rock and with God's amazing grace, we will share a life full of happiness. I love you so much."

As they looked into each other's eyes, the pastor pronounced that they were man and wife. Jack leaned down and tenderly kissed Krista then taking her hand they walked back down the aisle as everyone clapped.

The usual parade of picture taking took place while the guest headed for the Crescent Hotel. Soon they were boarding the waiting carriage. Jack could not take his eyes off Krista as the horses pulled the carriage toward the hotel.

"You're the most beautiful thing I have ever seen," he said staring down at her. With a thumb, he wiped the tear from her cheek and said, "I love you Krista, more than you will ever know."

"We are so fortunate Jack, God has blessed us and this marriage, I can just feel His arms around us. It was a precious moment when you said your vow to me and I'll always cherish it."

The carriage pulled up to the entrance to the decadent building. Jack jumped down and went around helping Krista down from the carriage. Holding her skirt in one hand and Jack's hand in the other, they climbed the stairs to the lobby. All eyes were on them as they went straight to the reception hall fully decorated in vintage décor representing an era gone by.

Smiling faces everywhere filled the room as the bride and groom entered. People from Rogers, neighbors, and co-workers alike were there. Townspeople that knew Krista and Jack, Jack's family, and of course the choir members and congregation from their church were there. The cake covered with roses stood three layers high in the middle of the table with the chocolate groom's cake in the shape of a cabin.

The band began to play and the newlyweds had their first dance as husband and wife. Jack leaned down and kissed Krista to everyone's delight. Encouraging one more kiss, the attendees kept clapping.

After a few more dances, Bud tapped the edge of his glass with a spoon to get everyone's attention. In the silence that followed, he found himself tearing up, clearing his throat he began to speak.

"Jack and I have been friends since grade school. We have been there for each other through thick and thin. No one could be happier to see Jack so happy and I feel like Krista is family, like a sister. Here is to a very fortunate couple that has found true happiness with each other, may this union last fifty, no, a hundred years," he said laughing.

As everyone raised their glasses, Bud noticed someone standing outside the double doors to the reception hall. Just then, Jack came to him and thanked him for his toast taking his attention away from the door. Turning toward the doors again the person was gone. He was sure it was Carrie. Not seeing her anywhere, he started to walk across the room, through the lobby, and outside. He saw her running through the parking lot and getting into a car. Before he could reach the car, she had pulled away. He stood breathless in the middle of the drive watching her disappear around the curve and out of sight.

Returning to the festivities inside, Bud watched Krista and Jack greeting people, laughing, hugging and an emptiness swelled in his being almost sending him into a place of extreme discomfort. He walked to the punch bowl and dipped the red liquid into his glass.

"They are happy," a voice from behind, stated.

"Yes, they are," Bud, said, turning around to find Betty. "I envy them."

"Your time will come, Bud, don't give up," she said smiling.

"Do you think so?"

"Yes, I do."

As Betty walked away, Bud pondered what she had said wondering if perhaps, there had been hidden meaning. He wondered if she was not telling him everything she knew about Carrie. *Why had Carrie come to the reception? Was it a coincidence? Had it been her intention to show up at the reception? Had Betty seen her too?* These questions lingered with him for the rest of the evening.

Mason came up beside Bud and whispered, "Are you ready, I have the cans in the back of Ben's car."

"Yeah, let's do it, now's a good time they're taking pictures again."

Bud, Mason, Brad, and Ben headed for Jack's truck. Getting the string of tin cans out of the trunk, they began to tie them to the bumper of Jack's new white F 150 pickup. They painted on the windows JUST MARRIED then filled the cab with balloons attached to the doors to release when the doors opened. Then they ran back to the reception trying to appear innocent of any childish prank. However, Jack had noticed their absences and headed their way.

"Uh oh…we've been caught…. Split up," Bud said strolling to the groom's table for a piece of chocolate cake.

"What have you been up to?" Jack demanded, standing next to Bud facing away from the crowd.

"Me? What have I been up to, nothing just getting a piece of cake," Bud said stuffing his mouth.

"Bud, that is a brand new truck, please tell me, you didn't ruin the paint."

"I don't know what you're talking about,"

"Sure you do, I know you way too well, and I'm just saying if the paint is ruined with your childish prank, you're going to get a bill from me."

"Now, Jack, go back to your lovely wife and stop worrying about that shiny new truck," Bud said with a grin as he walked away from the table leaving Jack to wonder if he dared to run out and take a look at his truck or stay with Krista.

The answer to his question came soon enough as Krista called to him. Walking up beside her, she smiled and softly told him she loved him and he forgot all about his truck

Pinks and oranges showed through the many glass windows surrounding the hall, announcing the arrival of the evening sunset as Jack and Krista made their way to the door followed by well-wishers. Still in their wedding clothes, they headed for the truck as a shower of birdseed fell around them. The site of the decorated truck stopped them in their tracks and they began to laugh.

"I feel so young, don't you?" Krista said as they continued to run to the truck.

Opening the door, balloons hit them, as Jack frantically untied them from the door handle letting them fly everywhere and head for the sky. Jack and Krista looked at each other and laughed again.

"I was hoping they wouldn't do this, but now I think it makes the whole experience that much more special," Jack said helping her get her dress inside before shutting the door.

As they pulled away, they waved to everyone out the windows. Then smiling at each other they headed for the cabin unaware of what was to come.

*****

The next morning Krista woke to the smell of bacon and coffee. After a night of noise from the rowdies, she was finding it hard to wake up. Finally, anxious to see her new husband she walked into the cabin's kitchen where she found the table set with flowers in the center.

"I could really get used to this," she said with her arms around his waist as he turned the bacon.

"Well, get used to it because it is going to happen more and more now that we are married."

Molly Owen

"We are married, aren't we, and I love being married to you,"

"Have a seat Mrs. Nolan and I'll pour you a fine cup of coffee and serve you the finest bacon and eggs you have ever had," Jack said, giving her a quick kiss on the forehead.

"Did you suspect anything, I mean about the guys last night?"

"No, that was a complete surprise, I think Bud probably had something to do with coming up with the idea, he has always had a wild streak. That's why he and Carrie got along so well,"

"Did you see her at the reception?" Krista said

"No, was she actually there?"

"Yeah, and Bud went after her, I don't think he caught up with her because when he came back he looked confused."

"Enough about Bud, I guess I'm selfish but I just want to talk about us," Jack said, taking her hand across the table.

A knock on the door startled both of them as they looked at each other in disbelief. Jack got up from the table and crossed the living room and opened the front door. Bud stood white as a sheet in front of him.

"What's wrong?"

Bud could not find his voice. Then he finally choked out the words. "There was a bad accident up on highway 62. It was Carrie…she's gone, Jack."

"Come in Bud," he said, leading him to the kitchen. "Here, sit down and I'll get you a cup of coffee."

Bud looked at Krista with tears running down his face. "I'm sorry, but I don't know what to do,"

Krista got up and went to Bud putting her arms around him. "It's okay Bud we're friends and we love you," she said looking at Jack as he poured a cup of coffee.

Krista and Jack sat down and waited for Bud to regain his composure. Jack reached over and squeezed Krista's hand. Finally, Bud began to tell them what had happened.

"While I was here acting like a schoolboy, Carrie was at the bottom of a ravine fighting for her life," he said in anger. "We got a call this morning about seven o'clock that someone spotted a car in a hollower with its light still on like it had slid tail first down the hill. When we got there the rescue squad was pulling the basket up a very steep incline." Bud stopped and took a breath.

"It's okay Bud you don't have to tell us. I'm sure it was a shock," Jack said, touching his arm.

"You don't know half of it. After we loaded the body in the unit, they handed me a purse. I opened it to get some identification and pulled out an envelope. It had my name on it.

Molly Owen

At first, it didn't register, so I kept looking for a driver's license, you know to find out who it was," he took another deep breath.

"When I found it, it was Carrie's. Carrie was in the body bag, and I fell to my knees,"

"Oh, how awful," Krista said, starting to cry. "I'm so sorry Bud."

"I'm the one who's sorry, Krista I shouldn't have come here. It's your honeymoon," he said getting up from the table and heading for the door.

"Wait, Bud, where're you goin'?" Jack said getting up and following him through the front door of the cabin and outside onto the porch.

"I'm sorry man. Forgive me, Jack," Bud said getting in his truck and shutting the door.

"Bud, it's alright. Don't you see? You came here because we are friends and we stand by each other no matter what. You need to be with us right now. Come on back inside. We wouldn't have it any other way. Come on Bud," Jack said, opening the truck door.

Bud laid his head down on the steering wheel. Then pulling an envelope out of his pocket, he handed it to Jack. "I can't open it. I'm afraid of what it says, you know? Either way, whether it is a 'Dear John' letter or something else it doesn't matter now."

"Come on in and we'll read it together. Come on Bud." Jack said, helping him down from the seat of his truck and walking with him to the front door of the cabin.

Krista had gone to the bedroom and changed out of her night clothes and into some slacks and a long shirt. When they came back to the kitchen, she was standing with her back to them making another pot of coffee. When she turned around Bud had his face in his arms on the table in front of him. Jack nodded and silently mouthed the words to Krista 'I love you.'

"The last time I saw her was at your reception. I think she wanted to talk to me or maybe she just wanted to give me the envelope. I went after her but she got in her car and was gone before I could stop her," Bud said, raising his head from the table.

The envelope lay on the table in front of Jack. Bud stared at it and shook his head. "Let's just tear it up," he said, reaching for it.

Jack did not move as Bud took the envelope and turned it repeatedly in his hands. Tears covered Krista's face as she watched the pain Bud was experiencing and remembered her own pain when she lost Drew. She was aware that Jack was feeling Bud's pain also as he remembered losing Debbie. The three of them sat in silence until the coffee pot buzzed. Krista started to get up but Jack motioned her to stay while he got up and coming back to the table poured each one a fresh cup of coffee.

Jack sat down and bowed his head. *"Father of mercy, we ask you for comfort and peace for our friend. In this hard time, put your arms around him, show him your love, God. Take away his anguish and his fear Lord, replace it with understanding and fill his heart with your grace. We thank you, Lord, for the gift you have bestowed on him. His ability to help others in a dire situation is such a blessing to us all Father and we are so grateful. Lord keep the Holy Spirit within him that gives him courage and the knowledge that you are with him always. In Jesus' Name. Amen."*

Bud raised his head and looked at Jack with disbelief. He had so many questions, so many things he wanted to say to God. *Why did this happen? Why couldn't I be there for her? Where were you, God?* These things pounded at his mind. He just wanted to escape from knowing, from not knowing, from the sadness that surrounded him. Finally, he tore open the letter and began to read aloud with anger and forcefulness.

Dear Bud,

I know you have wondered what was going on with me, and why I came looking for you. I couldn't make up my mind whether to tell you or not. It didn't seem fair to let you know I'm dying now that we could be together again.

I only have a few months to live and I guess I was being selfish but I wanted to spend them with you. I always knew you and I should be together. I'm so sorry I didn't wait for you. If you remember, I have always been impatient.

Please forgive me, Bud.
You will always be my first love.

Your Sweetheart,
Carrie

Bud stared at the paper. Looking at Jack, he asked in anguish, "Did she take her own life?"

"We will probably never know and without that letter, the authorities will never suspect," Jack said.

After a couple of hours and with a clearer picture of what was on Carrie's mind in her final hours, Bud thanked his friends and told them how important they were to him and to each other. They went with him to the door and watched as he got in his truck and drove off down the road. The only sound around them were the tires on the road leading away from them and an occasional bird singing it's morning song as if to say all is well. They walked hand-in-hand back into the cabin.

They made an effort to change the atmosphere around them and to enjoy the time they had together. That afternoon with spring in full bloom and a slight breeze in the air, they headed for the hiking trail behind the cabins. Both in their own thoughts, neither one said a word. They had been hiking for a while and came upon a resting area with a rock wall for safety overlooking the beautiful mountains surrounding them. Standing next to each other, they viewed the sight in front of them.

Molly Owen

"God is so magnificent, look at His wonderful creation," Krista said.

Jack stood in silence taking it all in. The fresh air filling his lungs and the love of his life filling his heart. He looked down at Krista and asked her to pray with him. *"Father, you are so worthy of our praise. We stand here in the vastness of your glory and thank You for blessing us and giving us your grace, Lord. Thank you, Father, for leading Krista and me to find each other and giving us a chance for a new beginning. We ask for your peace, your guidance and your blessing on our friend, Bud, as he begins his journey through grief, and Lord, give us the strength and patience to be his guiding light as he finds his way to you. Thank You, In His Holy name, Amen."*

Chapter *19*

The Inn was overbooked and Victory's was bustling with customers as the summer months filled Eureka Springs with vacationers enjoying the uniqueness of this quaint little town in Arkansas. Sidewalks filled with window shoppers, restaurants had lines waiting to get in to experience the tastes of different cuisines.

Nightly accommodations were booked for days ahead thanks to the wonderful weather.

Jack carried some boxes of merchandise into the boutique from the delivery truck. Dodging customers, he set them behind the counter while Krista signed the delivery sheet for the driver. They had not had a moment of rest since their honeymoon. They were so tired at the end of the day, which most of the time was late in the evening after making sure rooms were ready for the next guests when they went to their quarters they barely had time to eat dinner before going to bed.

"Our decision to live at the Inn was a good one. We would have never made it if we had to go home after a day like today," Jack said frying some bacon and eggs for their dinner.

"I know. Jack, I'm so grateful for all the business and I love seeing the guests so happy, but I never dreamt it would be so hard. It's a good thing we took those few days after our wedding because it may be a while before we are able to take any time off again," Krista said filling the toaster with bread.

"I think we need more help, especially on the weekends. We could put an advertisement in the paper and maybe post it to our website. What do you think?" Jack said, putting the plate of food in front of her.

"We should talk to God about this Jack. I'm totally overwhelmed, to the point of exhaustion. Prayer would give us some peace, don't you think? And Jack, we haven't been to church together lately. You have gone because of the choir but I haven't been there in three weeks," she said between bites.

"You're right, sweetheart. Let's put this in God's hands. I'll clean up here while you shower and before we go to bed let's have that talk with God," Jack said giving her a kiss on the top of her head.

He heard Krista turn off the shower so he finished putting things away, let Goldie out then checked the locks on the doors, turned out the lights and took his turn in the shower.

"Boy, that was just what I needed. It is amazing what a good hot shower does for aching muscles," Jack said sitting on the side of the bed.

"I know," Krista said, reaching over to turn out the lamp on her side of the bed. "It's like a baptism for the body, washing away the aches and pains of the day."

"I'm not sure how much longer we can keep up this pace. I'm not complaining, we are so blessed to have the Inn full to capacity but it is a lot of work. We just need more help," Krista confessed.

Jack realized that Krista was very concerned about getting help, but wasn't quite sure if it was because they lived in the Inn or because it was so much to keep up with. If they decided to live at his place they would have to have dependable help or it wouldn't work.

Perhaps Mason could come in and help on the weekends, Jack thought. He could stay with them or one of the rooms, but that would take one of the rooms out of commission. His thoughts were turning around in his head when he realized Krista was about to go to sleep.

"Let's pray, Krista. *Heavenly, Father, we praise Your holy name. Thank you, Father, for your blessings. Our future is in*

Molly Owen

Your hands, Lord. We ask Your guidance in our decisions about the Inn."

Interrupting, *"And Father, thank you for the blessing of a child."* Krista said half-asleep, raising her head and turning to look at Jack.

Jack turned over and turned the lamp on. Looking at Krista, he smiled then hugging her he began to laugh.

"Are you sure?" he said. "No wonder you have been so tired lately."

"I know, so now we have to find some help," she said, still in his arms.

"We will figure it out, Krista, I promise. I love you," he said.

The weekend was in full swing and the Inn was booked. Victoria was buzzing with customers keeping Krista and Jack busy checking people in and running the cash register. Elsa and Herman agreed to come in at lunchtime and give them a break long enough to eat. Krista told Elsa she was expecting, much to Elsa's delight.

"But you can't keep this pace up much longer, running up and down those stairs and cleaning the rooms," Elsa told her.

"I know, we are looking to hire someone, but as you know it isn't easy to find dependable help," Krista told her.

"I may have a solution. Let me check something out first and I'll get back with you," Elsa said.

Elsa, on Sunday, had talked to a single woman who asked for prayer concerning her situation. The woman, Emily, lost her job and was about to be evicted from her room above one of the shops for her unpaid rent. Elsa thought this may be an opportunity, not only for Emily but for Jack and Krista. However, before pursuing this, she needed to check Emily out. So she went to the shop where she had been working and talked to the owner. Come to find out they had filed for bankruptcy. They said Emily was an excellent employee, dependable, hard worker, and the customers loved her.

That was all Elsa had to hear. So she went to Emily and told her about the Inn and shop needing help and for her to apply for the job.

"Be sure to tell Jack and Krista that I recommended you."

Elsa said, putting the phone down.

Emily proved to be a very dependable employee and they decided to move to Jack's cabin. With an extra bedroom for the nursery, it made sense to call it home. Krista hated leaving the Inn. She had poured her heart and soul into it. But now she had another priority, one she was looking forward to. Since they didn't want any rooms to be occupied by Emily, they decided to let her stay in their quarters as part of her salary.

Everything was working out fine, or at least to Krista's satisfaction. She and Jack would come into town on Fridays when most of the guests came to check into the Inn, and Krista would help the guests get settled by giving them their key and information about the Inn and where their breakfast would be on the buffet in the hall. She would tell them about Eureka Springs' attractions and the best places to eat in town. Then she would send them on their way with a reassuring smile. When not helping check guests in, she would help Jack and Bud with where to put new merchandise for Victoria's Boutique.

Even though it was unnerving at times, not to go upstairs to the living quarters she and Jack had shared. She appreciated the excellent job Emily was doing. They had become friends, not only through the Inn but Emily also sang in the choir at their church.

As Krista's due date came closer, she was able to let go of the Inn and concentrate on her life with Jack and the coming birth of their child. They spent many hours decorating the nursery and putting Krista's touch on the place they now called home.

"Jack, wakeup, it's time."

ANOTHER BEGINNING

EPILOGUE

Bud had just brought a patient into the hospital when he got a call from Jack on his cell phone. All it said was we are here and the room number. Bud turned to his co-worker and told him to wait in the unit and he would be right back. Running down the hall, he remembered that winter day when he found Krista injured on the floor of Victoria's Boutique. Now she was back in the hospital but this time Jack was right by her side.

He crashed through the doors leading to the room where he would find them. Then seeing the room number that Jack had given him, he tapped on the door.

"Come in," Jack said.

Bud walked over to the bed where Krista lay holding a tiny baby. He leaned over and kissed Krista on the head.

"Good job. Does it have all ten fingers and ten toes," he asked, staring at the baby.

"It's a boy," Krista said.

"Wow, Jack, a boy. Jack junior," he said excitedly for his friend.

Jack smiled at the thought of a Jack junior, however, he knew Krista had another thought on the subject.

"Me. Why me? I mean I'm flattered but why name the kid BUD?"

"Not your nickname silly, your real name," Krista said with a grin.

"Yes, how does Jackson James Noland sound?" Jack asked.

"Are you okay with that Krista?" Bud asked.

"I'm the one that suggested it when Jack told me your given name," she said.

"Wow, I'm honored," Bud said, wiping the tears from his face.

"Do you want to hold him?" Jack said, lifting the baby from Krista and handing him to Bud.

Bud was speechless as he held his namesake in his arms.

"Did you notice his red hair, like his momma," Jack said.

"I think he will have blue eyes like Jack," Krista said.

Bud still didn't say anything. He just kept staring at the baby he was holding. Then gently he gave the baby back to Krista.

"So, Jackson James Noland it is, and we will call him JJ after his dad and his dad's best childhood friend," Krista said, smiling down at their baby boy. "And I expect you two to keep this little fellow out of harm's way. Don't even think about sharing with him the shenanigans you two got into growing up. Understood?"

"Yes, momma," they said, in unison, with grins on their faces as they looked at each other.